The Gifting

A journey through life and death

By Bill East

ISBN: 978-1-914933-36-3

I21 Publishing. Manchester.
www.i2ipublishing.co.uk

Copyright 2022

All rights reserved. No part of this publication may be reproduced, stored in a retrieval system, or transmitted in any form or by any means, electronic, mechanical, photocopy, recording or otherwise, without prior written consent of the copyright owner. Nor can it be circulated in any form of binding or cover other than that in which it is published and without similar condition including this condition being imposed on a subsequent purchaser. The right of Bill East to be identified as the author of this work has been asserted in accordance with the Copyright Designs and Patents Act 1988. A copy of this book is deposited with the British Library.

All advice and expertise offered in this book is given with best intention and, to the best of the author's knowledge, is correct and safe. As such, any actions undertaken by the reader because of information gleaned from the book are at the reader's own risk and must be in accordance with all current regulations pertaining in the country of residence. If there exists any doubt or lack of sufficient knowledge or training of the reader to perform said actions, professional advice should first be sought before embarking on any such procedure.

For Isabel

Acknowledgements.

My thanks to my Publisher, Lionel Ross, my brilliant editor (and thankfully, pedant) Roy Clayton and the incredible Dino Caruana whose cover designs are the *ne plus ultra* of cover designs.

The Lord giveth and the Lord taketh away.
Blessed be the name of the Lord
Job 1:21

The Christian God is a being of terrific character -
cruel, vindictive, capricious and unjust.
Thomas Jefferson

I'm eleven years old and it's very cold, in fact, it's starting to snow. The snow is falling, well more like floating, in small flakes, as though it can't make up its mind how to proceed. We're playing football. I'm not so good at football but I've run up near the goal. I'm not sure why. Suddenly the ball is passed from Dougie Poate to Phillip Grey who crosses it towards me. Well, it looks like he crosses it. I think he was aiming for the goal but it's wide of the mark and the ball rockets towards my face. I duck and the ball just catches my forehead. It hurts my head like buggery - as the rather colourful expression goes – because the ball is scuffed through over-use and it absorbs water and that makes it quite heavy.

To my surprise, the ball is deflected into the upper back of the net and from that moment on I'm held in high esteem.

Then it happens again...and again and again, *ad infinitum,* or until I choose to stop it and move on.

I'm in 'Phase One'

I'm going to try to document the background to all of this. I don't know how this will happen because I don't have a computer or a typewriter or even a pencil and certainly no paper. I'll dictate it...but to whom? There's nobody here with me but I'll still do it. It will be a kind of autobiography from 'beyond the grave'...not that there was a grave.

8

Chapter One   Early Days

My name is Michael Spencer Brooks. Friends call me 'Mike', sometimes 'Mick'. Never 'Mickie' or, worse, 'Mikey'.

I was born in the nineteen-fifties in England. I was an 'afterthought', although my mother said I was 'a gift'. I suspect I was really the result of an error in timing. Dad converted to Roman Catholicism so he could marry Mum and I suspect that 'The Rhythm Method' had been used for contraceptive purposes! It isn't foolproof!

I don't remember Mum and Dad ever going to Church, even at Christmas or Easter time, though I think Mum went to Church when she was younger.

Well before I was born, Mum and Dad moved to Putney. They bought their first house there. Previously they'd been living with Mum's parents. Dad got a job as a 'floor walker' in a chain store. It was like British Home Stores but a smaller group and was strongest in the North of England. I wasn't exactly proud of Dad's work. I liked Dad though.

My elder brother was born just before the war and my sister during it, and so, as the baby of the family, I was 'spoilt rotten' by my siblings.

Prior to their marriage, Dad had lived with his family in Richmond. Mum was from Bermondsey in southeast London and thought Dad's family were 'posh'. Mum was very beautiful and had the dark hair and eyes that spoke of her Italian heritage.

My earliest memories are not my memories at all. They are the memories of my elder brother and my sister and my parents and my grandparents.

They remembered three things mainly, which were 'before The War' or 'pre-War' - which were better than 'during' or 'since The War' - and the 'Depression' and 'Old Rover' the dog (dead). I don't think I had any very early memories that were my own.

My own first memories included Mr Churchill's funeral.

'The War' was a good thing in many ways, said my father particularly since it brought people together. It was 'all for one and one for all' according to Dad, and the 'gentry' joined in with the 'working man' in a common cause.

Having said that, I remember hearing about the 'Black Market' where you could get anything you wanted 'at a price' from the 'Spivs' who ran it. So, altruism wasn't universal.

Mr Churchill was a hero to my father, and I was christened with Spencer my middle name as a tribute to him (Sir Winston Leonard Spencer Churchill).

I was told that my paternal grandparents' terraced cottage in Mortlake, southwest London, was bombed and consequently destroyed early in the war and my grandmother, though perturbed by the loss of her home and contents, was devastated that a neighbour had 'crept in' after the event and stolen all the cabbages from her garden. Perhaps this was 'all for one and one for all' in action.

After 'The War' was over, there was an election and the heroic Winston Churchill was dumped for the Labour leader, Clement Atlee. My parents were not pleased, but in hindsight the result was probably to have been expected. Attitudes had changed.

Beef, if you could get it, was tough, bread was 'like cardboard', 'marj' (margarine - with a hard 'g' if you were 'posh') was substituted for butter, beer was weak, clothing was of low quality.

"It's not like what it was 'pre-War'!" said my parents and their friends, who never seemed to stop reminiscing about what to me were 'far-off days'.

"The War ended nearly twenty years ago, for Christ's sake!" I'd say but the only response I ever got back was from my Mum who'd say, "Don't blaspheme, Michael! It doesn't become you".

I remember Aunt Ethel, my maiden aunt - everybody had one of those, either by dint of sexual anomaly or their being 'left at the altar', although sometimes it was because of the death of a betrothed, in 'The War' - going on a 'charabanc' (pronounced 'sharabang') trip to the 'seaside' and bringing me back a shell, 'if only she could find it'. Somehow, I became confused thinking the shell would be one from a rifle or larger weapon and I was to some extent disappointed when the shell, which was eventually found in the bottom of my aunt's handbag, turned out to be a rather delicate seashell, a member of the 'thin tellin' group (yes, 'thin tellin' is a shell group) showing a pretty pink translucency. I have the shell still.

I had a very old Uncle Walter who was married to Auntie Lizzie. They weren't really my aunt and uncle though they may have been my great aunt and uncle. Uncle Walter was ninety-six years old.

I don't remember much about Auntie Lizzie except she was a bit overweight and complained frequently about her 'Lumbago'.

We used to go to where Auntie Lizzie and Uncle Walter lived with their daughter, Auntie Sal, who was married to Uncle Jim. Auntie Sal and Uncle Jim had a daughter called Veronica.

In the hallway on a table, under a glass dome were the medals won by Uncle Walter during the Boer War. Uncle Walter sat in an armchair with a high back. He smoked a pipe and had a spittoon, a small pot made of terracotta into which he now and then squirted or more likely, dribbled tobacco-stained spittle.

He had a tattoo of a snake on his leg. He would only show us kids the tail, which was by his ankle, but we could see that the snake wound around his leg. Auntie Sal said we didn't want to know where the snake finished up.

My first really vivid memories were of the new pop group 'The Beatles' and the protest marches to Aldermaston with the slogan 'Ban the Bomb'. The World was about to end in a nuclear holocaust.

I remember with a high degree of pleasure, comics like *The Dandy* and *The Beano*, with characters like *Corky the Cat, Desperate*

Dan and *Lord Snooty and His Pals*. As I got older, I swapped to *The Eagle* - more sophisticated (!) – with astronaut *Dan Dare* and his green alien antagonist, the *Mekon* backed by his storm troopers, the *Treens*.

Dad stayed with the chain store and was quickly promoted to Store Manager.

They say that most ex-soldiers don't like speaking about their war-time experiences, but Dad was clearly the exception that proved the rule. He talked until his dying day about 'The War', which he claimed to have spent 'dodging German bullets' in France, Germany, Italy and North Africa.

We didn't own a car and didn't really need one. Public transport was plentiful.

In 1947 – long before I arrived - India had gained independence from Great Britain. Dad thought this was a retrograde step, which India would regret. Nowadays I regard the whole concept of colonisation as iniquitous, though maybe that's too strong a word. The ex-colonies have largely proved less than successful.

West Indian migration to the U.K. started roughly at the time I was born and increased in leaps and bounds. Reaction to this was mixed in my family. Both sets of grandparents hated it, my parents 'accepted' it and I rather liked the idea.

I'm reminded of the TV production, *The Black and White Minstrel Show* where half the cast wore 'black face'; totally unacceptable today but innocently regarded in the fifties and sixties. Times change, attitudes too.

I was a bright kid and though pretty sure I'd pass the 'eleven plus' exam which would get me into a Grammar school, Mum and Dad decided I should take the entrance exams for a whole bunch of top schools as a sort of back stop. This I did and I passed the lot, which gave me a choice of academic location not generally enjoyed by my peers. I picked a school, I think on the basis of the uniform, and stayed at that establishment for three years, until we moved north to a small village near Manchester, because of Dad's work. He was still with the 'chain store' and had applied for a senior position, which would require a move to Manchester. It surprised him that he was selected. Mum didn't want to leave London and neither did I but the increase in salary with the new position was such that the move became unavoidable.

I was accepted as a student by Manchester Grammar, and there at seventeen took my 'A' levels, the passing of which would assist my entry into university. Unfortunately, or perhaps otherwise, I failed these exams and got a job. It didn't matter much since none of my family had ever gone on to tertiary education and it certainly wasn't expected of me. Or perhaps it was.

I got a job in electrical engineering and went on 'day release' for attendance at a Technical College. At the time, the belief was that electronics or plastics were the 'coming things' so I was roughly in the right area of employment, but I hated it. So I resigned and to my parents' disgust lived for the next three years doing odd jobs and existing 'hand to mouth' as was the expression, mainly in France but also in Italy and Spain. I learnt to speak French quite well and have a bit of Italian but little Spanish.

I was, for the majority of my time in Spain, 'stoned'.

Why did I tell you about my early life? Well, I suppose apart from the times I spent in other countries prior to my 'settling down', I'd had a rather boring, uneventful and extremely conventional upbringing which was typical of the group into which I was born. 'The group'? 'Lower middle class' would have been the category at the time, although not now. People nowadays like to believe that 'class' doesn't exist. They're wrong.

I think that making my early life clear is relevant to future events. The point being that after such a mundane life, I made sure that retirement would herald a new and much more exciting existence.

It seems strange to me now, but I don't think we ever socialised with other families, only with relations. I don't remember my parents ever being invited to dinner at a friend's house. I think that was 'the norm' in those days.

Come to think of it, they never watched me play any sport either, not that I cared because I wasn't very good, but the concept just wasn't fashionable then.

O tempora, o mores! Or some such.

Chapter Two   A Successful Career and some Tragedies

I was twenty-two when I returned to England, determined to 'settle down', which I did enthusiastically. I got a job with a radio manufacturer called James Ross and Co. Ltd, established in the nineteen-twenties by a Scotsman called Frank James Ross. Old 'Jimmie' Ross was still alive at ninety-one when I joined the company and I met him on a number of occasions. Nice chap but reputedly 'hard as nails'.

FM radio sets, which we manufactured, were highly desirable still and there were plans afoot to manufacture televisions - some prototypes had already been made - but we were 'bought out' by an American computer company based in Houston, Texas called Comptex (Geddit?). The American Company wasted no time in converting us to computer manufacture. Computers were physically huge things then and not capable of very much.

A lot of the employees didn't like the idea of the takeover, particularly since it involved changing manufacturing from radios to computers and some left the company, but those that stayed benefitted greatly and never regretted the decision. There were many that still believed the market for computers was limited and the concept of desktop machines in the home environment was the stuff of science fiction or wishful thinking.

I stayed. I got into the computer field right at the start and remained with the same company until my retirement. This might appear boring, unadventurous, 'unaspirational', and lacking in ambition but I disagree. I slowly made my way up the ranks and finished up as Sales Manager of one of the divisions. If you produced results, the financial rewards were impressive.

Valves were still being used in radio production when I started but transistors were taking over fast and then, of course, as computers became more sophisticated came chips, and microchips and everything got physically smaller and, in terms of capability, much more powerful but it wasn't until the 'eighties' that 'personal computers' came into their own! Hewlett Packard was, I believe, the first.

I learnt 'programming' and became very friendly with one of the U.S. instructors who had been seconded to the U.K. for a year. After a while, he introduced me to a friend of his, a fellow Yank who was running the U.K. sales team. His name was Winston Parseley, which he said was a good name for sales because everybody remembered it. He had a gorgeous wife whom I lusted after like mad but never *did* anything. Well, actually I did. I played 'footsie' with her under a pub table once, but I think she thought it was a joke and I didn't disillusion her. Good job I didn't because I remained friends with her husband, 'Win', who eventually said, "Look, why don't you transfer into 'Sales'? I'll back you. Much more money; you get a car allowance, and you make your own hours".

I had married an Australian girl and she too had earlier advised getting into sales, mainly because of the car. I was a presentable sort of chap, always wearing a suit, plain or striped tie, shirt white or a very soft pastel shade. Neat hair. A little bit behind the trend I suppose. Just the type Sales Managers were looking for.

So with Parseley's help, I moved into 'Sales'.

I got a junior position and they sent me on a two-week 'live-in' sales course. It was the first time a 'Course' had been run outside the United States and my fellow trainees were two Frenchmen, one German, two Australians a New Zealander and oddly a Canadian who surely would have been better suited to one of the U.S. courses.

I've never met such a bunch of 'tossers' in my life…the instructors, I mean. They do say 'Them as can, do, them as can't, teach', and they're spot on! I spent two weeks on 'The Course' being worked very hard at all hours and learning about 'budgeting', 'targets', 'empathy', 'positive thinking', 'asking for the order', 'making appointments', 'countering objections' and a hundred other things from those instructor 'wankers' who were so far 'up themselves' even their mothers couldn't have loved them.

In the afternoons we played volleyball which was meant to 'bond' us. It didn't!

Back at work, I learnt more from the other salesman after office hours in the local pub than I ever did on 'The Course'.

The problem was that I was allocated the 'rubbish' in terms of customers. There was a natural and understandable reluctance in the established salesmen to pass clients with good potential over to me.

After three years of marriage and two years in the Sales Department I seemed to be getting nowhere. I was earning reasonable money but owning a house seemed just beyond our financial horizons, so we moved to Australia. In fact, I was transferred - on my request - by Comptex to its Australian Division and Annie, my wife, simply 'went home'. It was a period where 'experience in the U.K.' still held a certain *cachet* in Australia. I played this for all it was worth, and it worked to my advantage.

Fortunately, the Australian operation was situated in Gordon, on Sydney's so-called 'North Shore' and we were soon able to put a deposit on a rather nice little house on a new land release in Belrose about twenty minutes from work with much the same distance to the attractive 'Northern Beaches'.

I said that the work location was 'fortunate' and that was true because Annie's parents lived in Melbourne, a city which I later discovered held no attraction for me. Besides, while my father-in-law was quite a 'good bloke' my mother-in-law was an absolute 'pain in the arse'. She never, ever shut up! So it was rather pleasant to have her never, ever shutting up around six hundred miles from where we lived. Annie visited her parents at least twice a year, particularly after we'd had the kids and so all I had to endure was the annual Christmas week at our place.

I spent the rest of my working life in 'Sales'. I was selling equipment, 'hardware' and industry-specific 'software', to senior managers who hadn't got the first idea about 'IT' or Information Technology. Not that we knew it as 'IT' then. That came much later.

I was selling efficiency. I was selling increased profits and ultimately, I was selling promotions for the purchaser. And in many cases, that's exactly what the purchaser got!

I made a lot of very good money too and despite the opportunities that presented themselves with some regularity for extra-marital affairs, I remained married to the same woman for forty-five years.

And then she died. It was a brain aneurism, and it was very sudden. One minute she was in the passenger seat of the car, telling me of some incident in which she'd been involved earlier in the day and the next, she was in the passenger seat of the car, dead. It took me a long while to get over that, but her passing was only the first of a series of disasters.

Our son killed himself on - or 'off', more correctly - his BSA Gold Star, a British motorbike which he'd 'done up'. It was a bit of a 'heap' when he bought it, but he did it up beautifully. It cost him a lot, of course, but he reckoned in the 'pristine condition' (his words) it was in, after all his efforts, it was worth quite a lot of money, and he was right, I checked with some dealers. Unfortunately, after the accident it was a 'write off' and worth nothing.

Then our daughter, who was barely twenty-one, married a black chap; an American who insisted on wearing very dark sunglasses inside the house. He seemed quite a nice fellow though and very respectful. They went to live in America, Washington DC, but we never heard from her again. We heard from Wayne, the black chap, though. Toni (Antonia), our daughter had left him after a very short marriage and went to live with Wayne's best friend, Freddy, another black chap although a bit less black by all accounts, in Portland, Oregon. Wayne was not best pleased, but he'd seemed to accept the situation reasonably well. I thanked him for the information, though he didn't have any forwarding address. Wayne said he guessed his friend had a bit more than him, by which I assumed he meant he was richer. Toni had always been a greedy girl.

I had the intention of visiting Portland to look for Toni although what would I have done if I'd found her? As it turned out, I didn't go, and I've had no contact since. It's been nearly forty years.

Perhaps she's dead.

Then I was made redundant.

Comptex, the company for which I still worked, was 'restructuring'. As it turned out I was quite pleased because I was only a few months off retiring, and I got a bloody good redundancy payout.

My sister had died of cancer. She'd never married, although she'd lived with a partner for many years. My brother, who was quite a bit older than me, and a bachelor, had died too. Heart attack.

My parents were long dead.

So, with the redundancy payout and the Company Superannuation money, I was quite well off though quite alone.

I suppose I was expected to feel depressed about my situation, but I didn't. I was offered 'counselling' by the company and took a great deal of pleasure in refusing the offer on the grounds that I didn't want some 'half-baked, twenty-year-old, snot-nosed, so-called psychologist' interfering in problems with which I was well able to cope myself. Some 'bright spark' in the company even entreated me not to 'do anything silly', by which I think he meant, no, I'm sure he meant, 'don't top yourself.' Why he didn't come straight out and say 'suicide' I don't know. Euphemisms abound at such times.

Patricide, matricide, fratricide and sororicide get rid of the entire family, except oneself. That only leaves suicide, which is a word whose etymology is partly the genitive of the Latin 'se' (self) i.e. 'sui' (of oneself). I learnt that from 'Wikipedia'.

But I'd contemplated suicide for reasons other than depression over my perceived loneliness and was of the firm belief that my demise would be thus achieved when the appropriate time arrived.

More of that later.

It was at about this time that I first became interested in the actor Mando Oliver who had played the character 'Castro Mulligan' in the British TV series, *Whipsnade*. I admired Castro Mulligan and would have liked to have been like him.

The idea of being able to re-constitute times of high and exciting emotion that had occurred during one's lifetime had considerable appeal to me. The difficulty was only my inability to recall some of the times of the incidents in question.

For the most part I had no clear impression of this problem since I knew and remembered the euphoric aspects of my life and mostly the times they occurred. Or did I?

I thought that I had complete recall of all my 'highs' but one day - I use the term 'day' to indicate a point in time, there are no 'days' here - I remembered the feeling I'd experienced when I suddenly mastered the art of skating. This memory came 'out of the blue' and I was unable to place it in terms of time or location.

I knew that I'd been going to the rink for weeks and was particularly unsteady still. Then, suddenly it all 'gelled' and I was sailing round the rink with confidence. Nothing flash yet, I hadn't even attempted skating backwards, although I was able to accomplish that after only a few subsequent attempts, but I was skating. The feeling was one of triumph and joy. No, more than that! It was euphoria.

I was able to re-live the experience over and over but the knowledge that I hadn't recalled the time or place worried me.

Something, or somebody, some superior being had given me the facility to re-live the high points in my life and yet I was accepting the capability in a rather cavalier fashion, where perhaps there should have been gratitude shown in some way; and the only way that I could conceive of that would be to recall *everything* - all the details - which I had thus far plainly failed to do.

Meanwhile I continued to re-live 'learning-to-skate-with-consummate-ease'.

Chapter Three   Retirement and Ambitions

Well, that's enough of history. What about the present? I was sixty-five with, I hoped, quite a few years ahead of me. What about the post-employment, widower future? What about something exciting, something extraordinary?

As I've said, the redundancy and the retirement pretty much coincided and I didn't resent that arrangement. It meant I got some more money out of the company; not a lot but it all helped.

Now, what was I to do to occupy my time?

Read the classics? Listen to music? Paint in oils? Watercolours? Golf? Bowls? Jesus, no! Get fat and play darts? Getting fat seemed compulsory if you wanted to play darts at the top level! Learn the piano? Possibly, but I thought my hands were fast approaching a lack of suppleness.

All predictable, anyway! And I'd already tried painting. It's easy! No, *really*! Any fool can paint, it's just like doing anything else. A few tips and a bit of practice and 'wooshka!', you've got it. Want to paint an eye? No problem. An ear? Hands? Plenty of famous artists never managed that but with a little bit of effort, anybody can do it.

The problem is 'artistry'. Personally, I think abstract art's crap but have a look at something by Kandinsky or Rothko or Pollock. You'll probably think, 'I could do as well as that!' Well, try it. Good luck!

Composition is the key to artistry. A 'feeling' for design is essential. Without it, you can't be an artist.

I knew that I could be a craftsman, but I'd never be an artist. You can learn craftsmanship, but you have artistic talent…or you don't. It can't be taught.

So painting was 'out'.

I remembered a purchasing manager at one of my bigger customers. I went to his retirement party. His life had been his employment, his whole being had been invested in the company for which he'd worked. Even in retirement he still saw himself as a 'Company Man'.

The poor guy went on a 'retirement trip' to Europe with his wife. They started the holiday in Edinburgh where his wife's family came from and after three days there he had a heart attack and died. I can remember thinking at the time, 'What a bloody waste! You work all your life, and they give you a gold watch (yes, the company for which he'd worked for over forty years actually still did that) and then you die. Fuck!'

What I needed to do was something that neither I nor those who had known me would ever contemplate my doing. As it turned out it was easy to think of a few possibilities - drug addict, revolutionary, pimp, sex maniac, thief?

'Thief'? That had a bit of a ring to it and was worth pursuing. What I needed to do was look at the possibilities and select the most exciting branch of the profession. 'Pickpocket'? That held a degree of *panache*, of romance, I suppose. It needed nerve, which I thought I could muster but it also needed dexterity, which I didn't have, and could not, I felt, develop. Besides, didn't pickpockets work in pairs? I had no partner.

'Cat burglar' came up next but that also held a few negatives. Those people, I thought, targeted 'high rise' apartment blocks. I was inadequate at climbing, and I was terrified of heights.

But the simple profession of 'house breaking' and burgling had appeal, especially if the occupants were present in the house. That was it! I would become a burglar and to that end I purchased the tools of my proposed trade…a jemmy, a sack - actually a cloth bag with a drawstring which I already had and that had contained a pair of shoes - some black jeans, a black sweater and, from a specialist adventure shop, a balaclava with total face covering apart from gaps for the eyes and mouth. I was surprised the balaclava had been available. Its availability seemed to be encouraging criminality. In addition to these items,

I bought from the chemist, a pack of surgical gloves that I thought I might wear under some black leather gloves.

I laid out the items on my bed and wished I had someone to share with me the joke that now presented itself. The 'sack' called out for 'SWAG' to be stencilled on its outside and where was my horizontally striped burglar's sweatshirt? I had no idea what I would use the 'sack' for, but I intended to take it with me. The archetypical burglar always carries a sack and…one never knows!

I was ready to 'rock and roll'!

Now to the location, the target suburb. I chose St Ives as being the most salubrious on the North Side, where I lived. I knew the area well and whilst it was not the richest in Sydney - the Eastern Suburbs seem to have that honour - it was a good, 'middle of the road' starting point.

I took a couple of weekends to carry out preliminary research ('casing the joint' one might say) and settled on a house about halfway along a quiet street. I'd contemplated a *cul-de-sac* but realised that by following that idea, I would cut my escape paths in half. No, I thought that the selected house was the perfect choice, and I became more convinced of this when I rehearsed my procedure a few evenings later and found the street to be totally calm and quiet. I intended to park my car in an adjacent street that ran past a nature reserve and travel between car and house on foot.

Further research told me that the occupants were in the habit of going to bed at around ten o'clock each night, reading for a maximum of thirty minutes and then turning out all the lights. There were no children and no dogs.

All was prepared but I'm a careful chap, always have been and I felt the need to carry out a final reconnoitre. This I did and it very nearly ended the project. As I walked toward the house - it was around nine-thirty on a warmish winter's night - a late model Mercedes pulled into the driveway, the garage door opened allowing the car to enter and the door closed behind it.

The driver of the car was the owner of the house, there was no other possibility, and he did not see me. I, however, saw him clearly and I nearly called the whole exercise off. He was wearing a skull cap, a yarmulke or kippa. Mr King, I'd discovered that to be his name, and presumably his entire family, were Jewish. I hadn't thought of that. Not all people with the surname 'King' are Jewish but many of them are. I did not want to appear anti-Semitic. Silly, I know, but there it is.

Much thought later and I'd rationalised the whole thing. I intended to steal something or things of value, that was certain, but I would return those items by mail at the first opportunity. The King house was, after all, my first target, a 'practice run'.

I timed my 'attack' for one o'clock on a Monday morning - probably the quietest time of any week - and I have to say, the whole procedure went like clockwork. The back door of the property was unlocked and allowed easy and silent entry - I had donned rubber-soled moccasins - and I heard the snoring of Mr and Mrs King as soon as I entered the kitchen.

I intended to move quickly to the bedroom and inspect the side tables adjacent to the bed…or were there beds? Two singles, perhaps? And were there side tables?

By this time, my eyes had become accustomed to the darkness. I couldn't see clearly but I could see clearly *enough*.

It was a large house, a mansion by certain standards and modern enough to be devoid of creaky floorboards or stairs.

I climbed the stairs with a confected calmness although my heart was beating strongly.

In no time I had entered the bedroom and was standing next to the unconscious Mr King. There was enough light - I suppose from the moon - to see a wallet, some small change and a wristwatch lying on the side table. I pocketed these and moved to the other bed. The Kings slept singly. Here on the side table was a 'treasure trove'. Mrs King seemingly had the habit of removing her wristwatch and most of her jewellery before sleeping and it was obvious from first glance that Mrs King - or more likely, Mr King - was no cheapskate. I pocketed the lot and left by the same door through which I'd entered.

I was astonished. It had all been so easy. At first, I thought that I had possibly missed out a step or two in the burglary. Had I completed the task? I had gained entry, I had maintained the utmost caution, I had been incredibly quiet, I had tested each step of the stairs for creaks before committing my whole weight, I had entered the bedroom slowly and carefully, I had paused to establish the occupants' position, I had picked up my 'prizes' with delicacy, I had been decisive and not been greedy, I had made my exit…no, I had done everything with precision and in a calm and considered manner. The plain fact was that I had been successful. There had been no steps omitted. I was a 'natural'!

I arrived back at my home in a 'cloud of elation', double-locked the front door, closed all curtains and emptied my pockets onto the bed.

There before me lay the 'fruits of my labours' and those 'fruits' exhibited a 'ripeness' beyond my wildest dreams.

The first thing that struck me was the size of the diamond in one of Mrs King's rings. I was no expert on gemstones, but it surely must have been a five-carat stone. What it was worth, I had no idea, but I was sure that 'many thousands' would not have been an unreasonable quotation. Her other two rings were clearly valuable too, an emerald, square-cut and surrounded by diamonds and a cheaper - I thought - white opal one, a beautifully fiery stone in a plain setting.

Both watches were Rolexes, his solid gold and very heavy, hers lighter but having a bezel encrusted with small diamonds. Both valuable.

Mr King's wallet contained an incredibly large amount of money, all in one-hundred-dollar notes that a quick count set at around three thousand dollars. Who carried that amount of cash on his person? Obviously, Mr King did. Was Mr King a crook?

Additionally, the wallet contained a small number of low denomination notes, a 'platinum' American Express card, two bank cards, a driver's licence and a score card from the Monash Golf Club, an examination of which gave the reason for the card's retention. Mr King was a low handicap golfer and the card showed three 'birdies' an 'eagle' and a 'hole-in-one' on a 'par four'. Impressive! Very impressive!

Mr King would get his score card back along with his other property and that of his wife, much though I was tempted to keep the gold Rolex.

I went to bed elated.

The following morning I packed everything up, addressed the package and drove to a Post Office two suburbs away.

I was about to enter the premises when I turned, went back to the car and drove home. I locked the front door behind me, went to my bedroom, closed the curtains, opened the package and removed the gold Rolex. I repackaged the remaining items and returned to the Post office.

Chapter Four   Not Quite so Professional

In a way, it disappointed me that the King project had been so easy. Initially, my ego had put the success down to my innate skills in planning and indeed, in carrying out the burglary but further consideration showed me that my success had been due to a fortunate set of circumstances that ran in sequence to facilitate my 'triumph'.

Subsequent burglaries would inevitably prove more difficult. Maybe the next one, maybe the third or the fourth but problems would sooner or later arrive. I made a mental note to avoid over-confidence.

So, what next?

I didn't move far from the area in which I had launched myself into criminal life. Wahroonga is a wealthy suburb bisected by the Pacific Highway, which largely follows a north south ridge between Sydney Harbour and the Hawkesbury River. I selected the Western side of the Highway. Frosts occasionally appear in this area, whereas St Ives is largely frost-free…I think…although I can't see the relevance of this fact, if it *is* one, to my story.

I chose as my next target a house on a road off the Comenarra Parkway. It was a *cul-de-sac*, which I'd thought initially should be avoided but as with the St Ives property, the occupants were a couple in their seventies with no live-in children and no dog. Added to which, I'd known the male occupant. I knew him in my life as a Sales Manager with Comptex. He was a customer who put me to a great deal of inconvenience and then bought from the 'competition'.

His name was 'Robbie' Mumford and I didn't like him. His wife was quite pleasant though.

I intended to steal as much as possible from Mumford. I wanted to take my revenge for all the inconvenience his inflated ego had inflicted on me during my working life.

Mumford was well known as a Freemason, which would have been reason enough for my not joining that organisation. My dad was a Mason and he once admitted to me that he'd thought becoming a 'Brother' might do him 'a bit of good' after his 'demob' from the Army after the war. He told me he'd been disillusioned in that regard but had stayed with 'The Lodge' because he enjoyed the company and that the 'otherworldliness' of the rituals had a sort of calming effect on him. "Besides," he had said, "they do a lot of good".

Just prior to my leaving for Australia he asked me if I'd like him to invite me to join but I told him 'No', which actually seemed to please him. Freemasonry had a small influence in the business world and in parts of the Public Service - the Police, I think - when I first arrived in Australia, but its influence has almost disappeared now. Mumford had hung on and was Master of his Lodge.

By great good fortune, I discovered that it was Ladies' Night at Mumford's Lodge the following Wednesday and in consequence, the Wahroonga house would be empty. So, next Wednesday it would be, and I was delighted meanwhile to discover that Mumford's house did not have an alarm.

Six-thirty on that Wednesday evening found me parked on a grassed patch at the side of the Comenarra Parkway. I was waiting for the Mumfords' car to appear. At six-fifty the pale-yellow Volvo, strictly observing the speed limit, passed me, Mrs Mumford talking, her husband looking grim and staring straight ahead. I left my parking place and drove to the Greengate Hotel at Killara on the Pacific Highway where I quite quickly consumed two schooners of beer and two packets of chips, then returned to the car and drove in the darkness back to the Parkway end of Mumford's street.

It always amazes me how quiet our suburbs are after around seven-thirty on a mid-week evening. I suppose in the more affluent suburbs all the 'bread-winners' are employed in jobs that finish between five and six p.m. and most are safely home between six and seven. A drink, some dinner and settling down in front of the television follow the homecoming and that's it until bedtime. Not exciting but understandable and for burglars, like me, targeting houses in the area, fortuitous.

I left the car and walked unseen to the Mumford house. I had worn a sort of anorak with voluminous pockets ideally suited to holding my 'swag' but discarded this item of clothing due to the warmth of the evening. I had pockets in my black trousers, but it soon became evident that the 'swag sack' would prove a useful item.

A raised pathway led to the front door, and I took that route taking care not to look too furtive but, at the same time, keeping aware of the possibility that I might be being observed, though as far as I knew, this had not been the case.

I inspected the door and discovered Mumford's security well catered for. There were three locks on the front door, one unengaged but the main one was locked, as well as a deadlock. Entry to the premises was not going to be via that portal but considering the easy entry possibilities it was essential that the backdoor be checked. It's amazing how many people will secure their property with much enthusiasm at the front whilst allowing easy access at the back.

I returned to the street, which appeared much as it had done previously; silent and unpopulated.

It was obvious that to access the back entrance to Mumford's house I would need to travel via the side and rear garden. It was convenient that the house was the last one in the street and the side of the property along which I should move lay adjacent to virgin bush.

I pushed through the murraya hedge and feeling confident now took a further step into the garden.

I stepped into an empty space.

I had failed miserably in my reconnoitring. There was a gully to the side of the Mumford house and the lawn was a part of its crest. I was furious with myself but fortunately unhurt by my impact with the ground. I looked up and judged that the drop had been nearly two metres, the lack of injury I assessed as being due to my relaxed body being unaware of the pending fall. I got to my feet and took a tentative step further onto what I perceived to be the lawn but was propelled further down the slope, which I had not realised continued, my initial landing being on a narrow terrace about a metre above the lower garden area.

I was propelled by gravity and a lack of spatial awareness onto the lawn and was forced into a rapid trot in order to regain my balance until progress was arrested by my arrival at a glass and timber 'garden frame'. I badly barked my shins on the surrounds of this structure and was thrown forward, smashing through the glass and timber cover, and landing in what turned out to be cucumber plants. I regretted my decision to discard the anorak, which would have afforded some protection.

In an attempt to break my fall, I had instinctively thrust my hands out, the palms forward. My hands were badly cut and blood was coursing down my face from one or several head wounds. There was glass everywhere, but no bones appeared broken. The noise of my accident had been loud, a dog was barking.

Panicked, I got to my feet and ran up the slope of the lawn, climbing onto the raised pathway. I ran to my car and drove home.

My clothes were torn and covered in blood. I felt sick.

I parked the car and let myself into my house. Thankfully, I had seen nobody.

I moved quickly to the bathroom and looked into the mirror, in horror.

My hands were becoming more painful by the minute and my face was a bloodied mess. To my amazement, a shard of glass was protruding from my scalp. I tried to remove this, but the pain was so intense that I vomited, missing the toilet bowl completely but hitting the seat and the surrounding floor. I would clean that up later.

My injuries amounted only to cuts and bruises, but they were severe. I should have gone to the local hospital to be cleaned and stitched but that couldn't be considered.

I laughed as I realised that the Mumfords would arrive home and perhaps would not see the evidence of my presence until the following day at the very earliest. The cause of the damage to their garden frame would probably remain a mystery.

But that was the only time I laughed for the next few days because my pain was excruciating although I believe it was made worse by my imagination. The thought of one's flesh being sliced has a sobering effect.

I assessed the damage.

I had two cuts on my face, one little more than a scratch, the other needing some form of stitching. A severe gash in my scalp, which was still bleeding around the protruding shard of glass and which would need some form of repair. Multiple cuts on my hands, which should at least be bandaged and very badly barked shins, which would have to be left to heal themselves.

Luckily, we had a 'first-aid' cabinet in our bathroom and it was always well stocked. I would set to as my own nurse, but first I'd strip off and have a shower.

This I did and the pain as the water hit my wounds was severe. Still, I persisted but the gash in my scalp proved more complex than I would ever have imagined. The pain when I merely touched the protruding glass was unbearable. There was still glass in one of the cuts on my face, though I was able to remove that quite easily.

The glass in my head turned out to be an 'L'-shaped shard the thickest end of which stood proud of my scalp The thinner and longer end had penetrated my flesh and channelled itself for about three inches between my scalp and my skull. I had not at first realised that this was the case. I could feel the protruding end and could see it quite clearly in the mirror but the resistance it offered to removal was immense. This had made me think that the shard had not only pierced my scalp but also my skull and was now lodged in my brain. I surmised that removal would only be achieved by surgical means and under total anaesthetic. Such an operation would be delicate and I might never recover.

I was concocting in my confused and possibly damaged brain a suitable story by which I could explain my predicament to a surgeon when it struck me that as I'd tried to remove the glass I'd experienced resistance but that the resistance had a sort of springiness. Perhaps the shard had entered at an angle and perhaps trying to pull at it in a direction perpendicular to my scalp was not going to achieve the desired result.

Back to the bathroom mirror.

This time I took the shard between finger and thumb and pulled forward. This new method was no less painful but was successful! The exiting glass seemed to go on forever - in fact, it was only a few inches - and as I slowly extracted it I felt progressively sicker until I had removed the glass completely, which was followed by a spurt of blood from the wound coupled with a stream of black vomit from my mouth, which landed spectacularly in the sink and up the bathroom mirror.

My cuts needed stitching but I had neither the skill nor the equipment to do that. Besides, I really don't think I'd have had the courage to do it even if I'd *had* the means!

In the 'first aid' cabinet there was a myriad of surgical items, analgesics, cotton wool, bandages, plasters of various shapes and sizes, tweezers, scissors, eye baths and so on but what I wanted was just two things…the scissors and a roll of 'breathable' adhesive tape. I recalled that the tape in question stuck 'like shit to a blanket' as the saying goes, and I would use strips of this material to suture my wounds. This I duly did and was more successful than I'd anticipated, although the end result of the scalp wound, which was nearly a centimetre wide in places might leave a lot to be desired once the plaster was removed (I anticipated ten days before removal, maybe longer).

I dried myself and went to bed, sick, exhausted and in pain. I continued to bleed from my wounds, but I had done all I could to avoid permanent scarring. Tomorrow would bring fresh thoughts and ideas.

Chapter Five   A Revision

Well, 'Tomorrow', did arrive but it included no new thoughts or fresh ideas, except for the fact that I would have left blood on the garden frame. Blood meant DNA and it would now, inevitably be in some police data bank. At that stage, the DNA would mean nothing, but I would need to be careful in my involvement with future misdemeanours.

I'd slept fitfully that first night, lying awake until around one a.m. mulling over my situation and then waking again at two, three and four o'clock to repeat the process before falling back to sleep. At five o'clock I had woken again and foolishly, taken a Temazepam tablet, or maybe it was two. These had helped, except that when I finally woke at eight thirty I felt 'groggy', out-of-focus and still tired.

In addition, in several places, I was stuck to the sheet!

It's part of the human condition, however, that 'It won't feel so serious in the morning' is a popular saying that holds true. How many times do we lie awake for hours worrying over some minor problem (which at the time doesn't feel 'minor') only to wake the following morning with the 'problem' greatly diminished and, moreover, frequently solved? It seems to be one of those truisms that really are universally true. Such a sentiment has been used in literature and song. Paul Simon used it in his song *Fifty Ways to Leave Your Lover*.

Sadly, in my current case the advice and its efficacy were very far from the truth.

The sliding doors of my wardrobe are mirrored and I stood naked in front of them. 'Embarrassing' would have been an inadequate descriptor if one only considered my physical appearance, but my overall reactions were also fear and shame.

I do not have the most impressive of figures and this, coupled with the many pieces of sticking plaster and the seepage of, now dried, blood gave me a clown-like appearance. There was a long cut down my back, which explained a lot of the sticking to the bed sheets, which I hadn't noticed before. How had *that* happened?

I did something I hadn't done since my teenage at the time of my first romantic rejection. I wept.

I thanked fate for having engineered my retirement and my lack of close friends. I had enough food in the fridge plus many cans and packets of nourishment in the larder to keep me alive for at least a month and assuming no unwanted infections occurred I could stay 'housebound' until my scars healed and, I hoped, faded. I felt thankful that I hadn't presented at the Emergency Department of the local hospital. *Staphylococcus aureus* is reputedly rife in such locations.

I collected the clothes, discarded on my return from my farcical adventure and, still naked, carried them to the washing machine. As I spread them evenly around the drum, I felt something hard wrapped in my tee shirt. To my surprise, I discovered a cucumber, rather squashed at one end, which must have entered my clothing via my neck at the time of the accident. I consoled myself that the loss of a cucumber was another indignity for Mr Mumford, a small one but an indignity nonetheless. An indignity for me too, really!

I took a bite out of the vegetable and tossed the remainder into the laundry's waste bin. I dressed and took stock of my situation.

Burglary had been...'fun' isn't the correct word because my second foray had been a painful disaster but it had certainly been an experience and it was one I didn't regret because it had told me something about myself, although not very much. Simply that I was capable of committing burglary, I suppose.

However, burglary was a career and that wasn't what I wanted. I'd had a career and I had no need for another.

No! I'd thought long and hard about it. What I wanted was excitement! I wanted to achieve things I'd never thought possible before. What I didn't want was to become involved in things that I could do without much effort…like burglary. When one thought about it, becoming a burglar was no different from any other job. Becoming a burglar was like becoming a postman or a bus driver or a shoe salesman in a shoe shop, all of less merit - for me, at least - than knitting a cardigan; knitting being a skill I didn't have and I'd have to acquire. Not that I wanted to knit a cardigan.

I made a list of everything that I thought might be worth trying to do. Things I could be proud of, things I'd need to struggle to achieve, things that needed thought, training and anticipation. Exciting things! What I'd do would be to make this list, then I would think about each item and get down to about three or maybe four things.

I suppose it *was* a 'bucket list' but I didn't think of it like that, and the reason was that the final thing on my list would be the bucket itself. I assumed that the term 'bucket list' referred to what you wanted to achieve before you died, i.e. 'kicked the bucket'. Now that's an interesting expression in itself. There are at least four explanations of the etymology (Wikipedia again!]), one at least dating back to the Middle Ages, but the one I preferred was the action of someone hanging themselves by 'kicking' away 'the bucket', on which they had stood, to arrange the preliminaries.

There was an excellent film on the subject, not suicide by hanging but about final ambition, about things - not necessarily significant things, not things that could prove of great benefit to mankind - that might be quite mundane but were of significance to the 'bucketeer'. It was called, appropriately, *The Bucket List* and starred the fellow who was in that superb film *The Shining* although his name escapes me. His friend was a black man, but I can't think of his name either. It wasn't Denzel Washington. Too good looking…well, in a way.

I just remembered the actor's name. It was Jack Nicholson, the white guy, but the name of his friend still escapes me. I'll go through the alphabet: 'A' no, 'B' no, 'C' no and so on right through to 'Z', with no luck. 'M' made some kind of memory jog but maybe 'P'. Oh yes, 'Freeman' which is neither 'P' nor 'M' but what was his second name? Black people in America seemed to adopt surnames - like 'Freeman' - as Christian names although 'Hoagie' Carmichael, in the nineteen-twenties, was white and his mother had had him christened 'Hoagland' after a railroad surveyor, Harry Hoagland, who was boarding with one of her relatives. Wikipedia doesn't agree with this derivation but they're not always right! I think the mother thought Harry Hoagland to have been 'successful' and copying his name might make her son successful too. Maybe black people did it for the same reason. Anyway 'Hoagie' Carmichael *was* successful as it turned out. He wrote lots of good songs including *Georgia* and *Stardust* which, in my opinion, was the best song ever written. I'll have to write to my daughter's 'ex', Wayne - is that another surname? - to get his opinion.

Anyway, it just came back to me. It was Morgan Freeman. Still, once again, Morgan is really a surname.

But back to my retirement ambitions.

Here's the list I made:

Do a Bungy jump
Do a parachute jump (solo)
Learn to fly a plane (solo)
Kill somebody
Swim the English Channel
Drive a car in a Formula 1 race
Run a marathon
Climb Everest
Get my gliding licence
Learn Mandarin
Write a novel
Kill myself, spectacularly but privately and cleanly

I thought about my list for a day or two but didn't take much longer than that to reach some conclusions. Items 1,2,3 and 9 were deleted first because, let's face it, anybody could do those things as long as fear was overcome and I'm not sure I could overcome my fear...or if I *could*, then the thing would be too easy. I really didn't think I could ever overcome my fear of Bungy jumping and the terror of any kind of stall in a small plane or a glider - essential for proof of competence before receiving one's licence - would have made items 3 and 9 impossibilities. I knew this because I'd been a passenger in a small two-seater plane where the pilot had proudly shown me the manoeuvre. I was terrified. Definitely not for me!

I was unsure if learning Mandarin would be viable for someone of my years and in any case, what would have been the purpose? To order food in a Chinese restaurant? They'd probably all speak Cantonese anyway. Writing a novel would be something anybody could do. But would it be any good? No point in writing a novel if it's no good. A novel might take two months or twenty years. If it turned out to be crap then it could involve a great deal of wasted time

So that left 4,5,6,7,8 and 12.

Well, 12 was non-negotiable. It was something that I *would* do, and I'll explain why later.

Climbing Everest and Racing Formula 1 were both things that would likely be impossible. Both pursuits were strongly controlled and again, age would tell against me. Did I have the lung capacity for an Everest climb or the nerve and super-fast reactions for a Formula One race? In both cases I doubted it.

I was a good swimmer and I reckoned I could, with training - a lot of it - swim the English Channel. It had been a boyhood dream of mine. It's on a par with the Marathon but a) it's lonely, b) it's cold, c) there aren't many spectators and d) you can never be sure what's in the water, or indeed, on top of it.

I remember, when I was about eight, we went on holiday to Broadstairs or maybe it was Littlehampton and I did some swimming lessons with a young blond chap, a 'lifeguard'. I think my mother and my aunt, who were with me and my sister, quite fancied him.

Dad wasn't with us though I'm not sure why. I'm not sure if my brother came with us either. Anyway, this lifeguard chap said that if I kept up my swimming, one day I'd swim 'The Channel'. I've always remembered that.

But 'No', I thought, on balance, a marathon foot race would always win out over a marathon swim. The adrenaline rush as one approached the final straight would be amazing not to mention the adoration of the crowds on the way around. So that's what I'd do, and the second thing would be to kill somebody.

My short-list of three things would therefore be:

To run a marathon.
To kill somebody (possibly after 'dishing out' some humiliation).
To kill myself spectacularly but privately.

Now, many would have said that a marathon at my age was an impractical aim. I'd be nearly sixty-eight in two years' time, and I'd never run long distances before. As a matter of fact, I didn't ever remember running competitively at any distance except at school where I was usually second last in any distance I attempted. Well, I didn't really attempt any of them. I was *made* to run by some kind of sports master, probably a paedophile, though I have no evidence.

I seemed to remember the name Brassington as being that of my usual follower who generally panted heroically and claimed quickly before I could offer such excuse that he had experienced a 'stitch'. Brassington seemed to regard his lack of sporting ability with a degree of pride, but it was quite the reverse for me. I *wanted* to be a sporting hero but was 'rubbish'.

I do remember fantasising about becoming a competent javelin thrower. I suppose javelins are made of carbon fibre now, although maybe not. Anyway, when I was at Manchester Grammar they were made, I think, of aluminium. My first and last attempt at throwing a javelin was thwarted by my failure to hold the spear in the direction of the throw. It felt right but in fact, as I took my arm back prior to release, my hand must have unconsciously assumed the angle necessary to throw a stone with the result that as I hurled the weapon forward, the rear part hit me with much force on the rear of the right side of my skull. Surprisingly, the resulting physical hurt was more painful than the embarrassment though I never tried it again.

I did attempt pole-vaulting but achieved nothing except a badly bruised shoulder and no lift at all, as the pole hit the 'box'. I *think* it was called the 'box'.

Cricket, a sport I loved, was purgatory to play, the ball being so damned hard and rugby, my winter sport of choice, meant frequent and painful bruising.

I didn't like team sports anyway. I'm not a 'team player' sort of person.

Of course, running in a world-famous marathon was going to be hard work and I expected to take a full year in achieving the necessary fitness. I knew - yes, yes, yes, I *knew* - that I'd have to be very careful. Muscle and bone and sinew become fragile as one ages and healing takes much longer. I'd always been amazed by young professional rugby players who, for example, break their back and then issue a 'press release' to say that they'd be away from the team for at least a month. I'm exaggerating, of course, but Christ, if it had been me, I would have been away forever. I'd probably have died.

Chapter Six   A Fruitless Exercise

It was while I was in my reclusive healing period, that I started thinking more seriously about the Castro Mulligan character. I got out the DVD set of *Whipsnade* again and studied Mando Oliver in more detail. If only I could be like him.

Well, I would *try* to be like him by, first of all, looking like him.

As soon as I felt better after my failed burglary - this took about ten days - I stopped shaving. I needed a neatly trimmed beard and moustache and whilst I was well aware that the colour would be wrong, I could, I thought, rectify that by the application of black hair dye.

Unfortunately, I didn't grow a thick beard and I found out to my chagrin that the growth was irregular and in some patches quite sparse, even non-existent, although the new-grown whiskers coupled with the scars did give me a rather sinister appearance.

Whilst this was exactly what I'd wanted, the beard would have to be forgotten.

By contrast, the hair was a success. I didn't suffer from baldness and my hair grew thick and straight. Perfect. The colour needed changing and change it I did. I bought a bottle of black dye and set to. After carefully reading the instructions on the packaging I applied the solution and the change of colour was spectacular.

The problem was…I looked ridiculous.

Why I thought the project would be a success, I really don't know. The hair had become a beautiful deep, deep black but the contrast between the hair and my white and freckled skin was, to say the least, comical. The effect was exaggerated by the fact that I hadn't thought to dye my eyebrows, which remained a light ginger. I blamed my father's Scottish heritage for that. Well, at least I wouldn't have the eyebrows to deal with.

I needed to come to the obvious conclusion and admit that I was being foolish. To do so, however, even to try, engendered feelings of disloyalty. 'Disloyalty to whom?' I'd ask myself. 'To Castro.' I'd reply. To Castro? To *Castro*? To a TV Series *character*? Quite ridiculous but for me to accept reality, to accept the truth wasn't going to be easy!

I thought it a great piece of good fortune that I was retired and could therefore extend my seclusion in my home or wear a hat if necessary.

I shaved my head, all the while being careful of my head wound. I looked even less attractive with a shaved head than with a hairy head but no matter. The problem was that the dye had coloured my scalp irregularly so that I looked not only like a sufferer of alopecia but also that my disease had been coupled with some kind of pied pigmentation of the scalp.

I wore a hat - it had become essential - generally a 'beanie', for two months, by which time the hair had grown to a respectable sandy 'crew-cut' and the scalp's discolouration had largely disappeared.

My self-doubt gradually diminished as my true pigmentation returned until finally, I was able to face life with some degree of confidence, although the scars from the cucumber frame were still evident and I have to admit that my scalp wound would have benefitted more from professional attention than by my own ministrations with sticking plaster.

I left my house and went for a walk. Nobody I passed took the slightest notice of me.

It is, I suppose an illustration of the 'otherworldliness' of my current situation that I can laugh at the actions of my mortal self. It's as though I'm now totally divorced from that person, that I feel no empathy towards him.

'What an idiot!' I think, without qualms, without embarrassment. What an idiot, indeed. Amazing that such a thing as the cucumber frame incident could have occurred! What was my mortal self thinking? Had I found it too irksome to properly plan for the burglary?

My current mind had difficulty 'coming to terms' – an expression I don't like – with the stupidity.

Has my intelligence increased? It doesn't seem so. And yet...

Chapter Seven   On Suicide

I was worried now, that the concept of a 'bucket list' was not new. Yes, there had been a recent - or relatively recent - film on the subject but surely the idea must have been considered by previous generations.

Why did that worry me?

Well, the answer to that was simply because I liked to be original. I knew no one who had taken the same course - except in the film - but what I meant was did I know of any of my friends or colleagues who had done so? The immediate answer was, 'No'.

But I wasn't convinced.

Perhaps a small percentage of people (I say 'people' because I try to encourage my thinking in terms of both sexes; I am, after all a great supporter of feminism) had done so after retirement or after having been told of the occurrence of a terminal illness; perhaps a significant percentage, perhaps most people, perhaps everybody. I suspect the latter but certainly, few have carried the proposition through to completion.

But some will have done so. Surely?

The reality was that those who have indeed put together a 'bucket list' would have included things that had been put to one side during their lives as being 'low priorities' and to a large extent these things were rather… I'm not sure of the most appropriate word but 'Kitsch' springs to the fore. I mean such ambitions as 'Having coffee on the Champs Elysée', 'Watching a sunset at Malibu Beach' or 'Swimming with the dolphins at Monkey Mia.' Yes 'Kitsch' is the correct word.

The thing that gives me comfort is that I strongly suspect few have included homicide or suicide in their programmes.

Actually, I'm not too sure about suicide, now I come to think about it. It's likely to be true that most people have considered it, although not many will have carried it through to conclusion, which is, as they say, 'passing strange'.

Why so? Because it's so easy. It doesn't have to be violent. In fact, there have been avenues open to potential suicides in various countries around the world which provide peaceful, respectful and entirely civilised methods with no pain involved at all.

I'm convinced that in the fullness of time, all countries will adopt 'assisted suicide' laws. It's coming, and as an indication of how attitudes have changed in my own lifetime, who would have thought that devoutly Roman Catholic countries like Eire or Italy would ever approve of 'abortion', let alone 'abortion on demand'.

Or 'Gay marriage'.

I have to admit that, at the time, I was somewhat ambivalent about both matters, but I don't suppose the sky has fallen in as a result of either.

Actually, I'd done some research (with the accent on the second syllable, please!) into suicide with some surprising revelations. Men are twice as likely to commit suicide when compared with women. What does that tell you? That women are more sensible than men. That men are driven to suicide by women? That women are less prone to depression? That men are braver? I could reach no conclusions.

I had thought too that suicide would be more likely to occur in the less 'liveable' countries but was again surprised that Australia came in at number 51, New Zealand at number 53 and France, my choice of country after Australia at 48.

Apart from Trinidad at number 43 all the other Caribbean islands, with hardly the most enviable standards of living, were way down at between 179 and 183. Perhaps it was the 'ganja'!

But what about historical figures, artists and 'celebrities?

Periander, Cleopatra, Socrates, Ernest Hemmingway, Sylvia Plath, Virginia Woolf, Rommel, Robin Williams, Kurt Cobain to name but a few. Why?

The answers vary; 'drugs', 'defeat in battle', 'depression', 'onset of illness', 'State diktats'? There was always a reason. Yet none, apart perhaps in the case of Hemmingway, for no reason other than the desire to do it and none, seemingly as the result of something that might or might not happen and none as part of a 'bucket list'.

    I have to admit that on hearing that someone has committed suicide for no apparent reason, I suspect an imminent revelation of hitherto unknown homosexuality. Maybe this suspicion is caused by bigotry.

I'd never previously considered the possibility of life after death. As far as I was concerned, when you died that was the end of it; all feeling, all consciousness stopped. You didn't go into Heaven or Hell or some neutral parallel universe. You were dead. That was it.

Yet here I was.

But where exactly was I?

It didn't seem to be a 'place' in the accepted sense of the word and yet I was here. Wherever 'here' was.

There was no time, no space, no up, no down, no distance, no proximity, no hot, no cold, and yet...

And yet, I had been given - by whom? - the ability to re-live actual events from my terrestrial life and in this non-physical 'place' in which I now existed I had retained a physical form and something, someone, had told me that my physical form was transmutable.

I sensed there was an ever-present possibility that I could change physically to become another person, or maybe an animal. I'd quite like to be a bald eagle; powerful, at the top of the food chain, with no predators and protected by the U.S. Government. What could go wrong?

It seems I know everything. There are no 'others' here, yet I know I'm in 'Phase One' and that there are three phases. *How* do I know that?

When I first arrived, I expected to be 'interviewed' and probably judged. I expected punishments but there was nothing and after a while it became obvious that the misdemeanours of mortal life held no relevance in this rarefied environment. Even the most serious of 'crimes' bore no significance. It was as though 'God' or whoever or whatever it was that controlled this place, if indeed this place is controlled by anyone, considered humans as being at a level such as humans might consider amoebas.

Chapter Eight   A Training Plan

I joined a gym, which came as a surprise to me - I mean the decision to do so - since I'd previously regarded such establishments as rather below me.

There were 'personal trainers' available but I thought 'I'll just do my own thing until I reach a level of competence commensurate with such training. 'Softly, softly catchee monkey' and all that.

'The Gym' - that's what it was called, for Christ's sake - wasn't cheap but I qualified for marginally lower rates because of my age and I have to say that the facilities were superb.

So here was my programme:

First, well, I'd try it to begin with at least, I'd exercise every other day because at my age I'd need to repair any physical damage I'd done during my exercise days. I was pretty sure that was right. Actually, I don't think damage is the correct word. I think you need a day to recover from the previous day's efforts and build the muscle fibre that your exercise has encouraged. I thought that was logical but if it wasn't, so what? That's what I'd decided to do.

For the first month, I'd just do gym work at 'The Gym'; weights and machines and stuff like that. Sometimes I'd finish off with a swim in their excellent pool, but I knew my shortcomings and if I did much swimming, at which I was quite competent, the next thing you knew I'd have been wanting to buy a bike and do some road work because I'd have changed my target to 'triathlon'. I could not afford to change my target. I would not. There was no time. My target was a marathon.

Now, in the second month I'd start running. Nothing flash. Maybe one hundred metres to start with on the first day, then I'd build up by adding a hundred metres each day. I thought about that; maybe alternate days would be safer. In ten runs I'd be up to a kilometre and after a year, doing alternate days, I'd be up to, say, one hundred and eighty times one hundred which equals eighteen kilometres (surprising!) That would be enough, nearly, for a half marathon although after the first year I'd add, say, five hundred metres each week. Of course, that was only a rough guide, there was no way, as I progressed, that I'd be able to run thirty or more kilometres every other day. Nevertheless, sticking to this 'rough estimate' would give me the competency to tackle a full marathon after two years, which I realise is one year longer than the single year originally envisaged but that didn't matter. Time, so long as disease didn't visit me, was on my side.

That was the theory! In practice, it was radically different. I would often need more than one rest day between long runs; sometimes as much as a week.

Maintaining enthusiasm would, I knew, be very hard and it could easily be the most difficult thing of all. Getting out of bed at five-thirty, in the dark on a cold winter's morning in order to do a road run or head to the gym would be an effort in itself and I would really have to steel myself to do it. In fact, I overcame the dislike of doing so by the simple expedient of regarding the action as part of the training itself. I would visualise getting out of bed early as equivalent to lifting a weight ten per cent heavier than that which I'd managed to lift the previous week. Ultimately, that seemed to work and getting up early soon became a habit.

I was nearly sixty-eight by then and if this project was going to take me as much as *three* years, so be it. I wasn't going to rush it. Besides, I could die in the next three years. No, three years might be more sensible and it would mean that I could do my first marathon at seventy or seventy-one.

Quite an achievement I'd say!

Meanwhile, I did some rough planning for the second thing; nothing too spectacular, just blurred outlines. The third thing needed very little planning because anyone could do it providing they had access to the means - a gun, poison, explosives, a car, a high building, lots of options - although I was going for explosives. An explosion would be more spectacular, although I had no intention of sharing the spectacle with anyone. I was thinking 'Manitoba'. There was a big lake there, which would be ideal, and Canada had the advantage of being some distance away from Sydney - and they spoke English.

Anyway, back to the project in hand, the marathon. Of course, as soon as you embark on this sort of thing you discover options you never would have dreamt of. There must be thousands of books about running and hundreds of computer 'apps' too. Some of these items were, as was to be expected, useless, but there was some useful stuff available.

I downloaded two books onto my 'Kindle', both written for the newcomer to marathon running. Both well and clearly written and both with the general message that launching oneself into this somewhat esoteric sport is acceptable at any age. That was what I wanted to hear.

The books told me that the principal consideration, apart from the necessary fitness, was 'shoes'. I immediately went to a specialist running-shoe shop in the city to get further advice and to buy the shoes to which my age, stature and feet were best suited. The first thing I noticed was that the sales staff were, or seemed to be, all runners and they were most encouraging. The second thing was their professional approach. I was put, minus shoes and socks, onto a sort of treadmill and a video was taken of my moving feet from all angles. The shop assistant, an extremely fit looking individual, told me that a simpler method of assessing 'pronation' was to stand on a wet patch of water and then make an imprint on a dry surface, but the video system was much more accurate, it could show up other 'problems' and would cost me nothing. I took this statement with a 'pinch of salt' because the cost of the machinery would surely be offset against an increase in the cost of the shoes. This shows me to be somewhat cynical, though realistic.

I was told that my 'pronation' was minimal and that this was probably due to my rather high instep. The fact that I pronated minimally had, apparently, a big influence on the kind of shoe I needed. I bluffed my way through a discussion of 'pronation', which, I understood simply meant the turning or rolling of the foot and the degree to which it rolls. They told me that I would best be served by having two different pairs of shoes, one for training in the gym and one for racing and told me that they needed to assess the 'drop' - which is the correct expression for the optimum height difference between heel and toe - before offering me a limited choice of the two shoe types. My 'drop' had been duly assessed.

The 'trainers' were more cushioned than the 'racing flats' and allowed for more varied movement while the 'racers' were designed simply for running. The racing shoes were unbelievable light.

The shoes cost me quite a bit of money, but I had plenty of that and I needed all the help I could get. The old 'Dunlop Volleys' didn't get a look in!

One of the web pages I stumbled across was that of the New York Road Runners; excellent stuff and for certain people, perhaps the majority, a very helpful resource. They offered to organise your training, your diet and so forth and they'd help you with your attitude, your emotions and pretty much everything you needed.

I decided not to make use of this resource or any other because I wanted to do the three things all by myself. This paints me as a stubborn fellow, I know but that's the way it was going to be. I would read books, though…but only if relevant.

It seemed foolish at the time - and indeed, when I thought about it later, it still did - but I tried to take on the persona of 'Castro', Mando Oliver's character in *Whipsnade* in all my training. Yet, the funny thing was, that it seemed to work. 'Castro Mulligan' was a fiction but the more I 'became' him, or at least, tried to think like him, the easier my training became. 'The Power of Positive Thinking'? Yes, I suppose it was.

I said, a little while back that I'd explain the reasons for my proposed suicide and I will, but not yet.

I'm not going to put this in the 'autobiography' because it's somewhat embarrassing, but I have to say that once I'd joined 'The Gym' I became completely involved in the 'fitness' concept. I started to look upon myself as in some way superior to 'non-gym' people.

I think this is not untypical. Humans like to be 'club members', it gives them a strong sense of belonging. It might be a political party or a religion or a club proper (gentlemen's, sporting, philatelic, business, charitable etc.) but whatever it is, I feel it's a weakness.

Yet, on the other hand, there are some who possess a sense of superiority by *not* having a gym membership, and *not* being part of the 'herd'. These same people are also often inordinately proud of having no involvement in 'social media' or depending on their political persuasion, refuse to buy or even read *The Australian* or *The Age* or *The Guardian*.

I think that my mortal form fell somewhere between these extremes. I'd been a contributor to *Facebook* but had later cancelled my membership (too many photos of people's lunches) yet, on the other hand, was happy to read the *Sydney Morning Herald* (*à gauche*) as well as *The Australian* (*à droite*). Each of us is different. Do these thoughts have any relevance to the autobiography I'm writing or dictating or thinking? It's doubtful.

Chapter Nine   Beginning Training and Some History

So, here I was. Day one. I hadn't thought of the 'Castro' system yet!

I went to the gym or 'The Gym' as they fancifully called it and checked out all the machines after being given an introduction by a quite attractive girl who, unfortunately, started every new statement with 'So...' and kept talking, with the fashionable 'pitch raise' at the end of each sentence. Can this awful habit be 'sheeted back' to the Welsh, or New York Jews, or is it simply a plea for reassurance? She lectured me, to the point of boredom, in this manner, about 'vulnerability' (which seems to be the accepted pronunciation nowadays) of muscle tone with regard to 'overdoin' it'. Then she left me, thankfully, to my own devices.

There was a sort of quiet area, which had all the equipment - machines and free weights - that I was going to need and I used it for the first month. This area had the advantage of being away from the muscle-bound, self-obsessed 'tossers' upstairs in the 'serious' area but the disadvantage of being somewhat less inspiring from the point of view of female scenery, not that *that* would have worried me at all. Although I was later to discover that as I progressed in my training and developed muscle, and nearly regained the figure I had twenty or so years ago, I welcomed the furtive glances of the opposite sex. I moved upstairs.

I started with low weights and increased in minimal degrees over the month. This seemed to be five-kilo increments for the machines and two-and-a-half kilos for the free weights.

Now, what I want to avoid in telling my story is the danger of boredom on the part of the reader, but there are two things that I've found very interesting in my research of the marathon and I think they both justify inclusion here.

Number one is the history of the marathon. Apparently, the distance of a standard marathon, which is twenty-six miles and three hundred and eighty-five yards or forty-two point two kilometres, is the distance between Marathon and Athens in Greece. This was the distance covered by a Greek message-runner, a soldier called Pheidippides when he took news of the Athenian victory over the Persians from the battlefield at Marathon to, presumably, the anticipatory throng in the capital. Pheidippides's message was 'Victory', or 'Nike' in the Greek language. He delivered his message and dropped dead. Well, that's the legend, although it's worth noting that Pheidippides had reputedly run to Sparta and back, a total distance of 280 miles in a failed attempt to get the Spartans to help just prior to the big battle. It's doubtful that twenty-six miles would kill a fit, athletic soldier but three hundred miles in the space of a few days would certainly have left him buggered.

The first modern marathon was run over the traditional distance and so has every true marathon since that time.

The second interesting fact concerns the famous 'Wall', which is the 'barrier' experienced by most runners at some time in their careers.

The body needs energy to function in any action and running takes a heavy toll on this energy. Energy in the body is supplied by glycogen. I had no idea what this substance was or how it was produced although I believed the precursors were sugars, carbohydrates, fats; stuff like that. The problem is that the body's store of glycogen is finite and after you run out of it, you have to rely on your fat store, which of course isn't that large in most runners and in any case the efficiency in using fat as an energy source is not very good.

I wasn't yet exactly sure at what point 'The Wall' was reached. Whether it was when the glycogen runs out or whether it was some way into the fat burning process I didn't know, but when you reached it, it was apparently a bit of a shock.

I started on the running after a month at the gym. A hundred metres is what I'd planned but a hundred metres seemed totally pathetic after getting my fitness up in the gym

('The Gym') during the first month. Still, I decided to stick to it and before I knew it I was up to a kilometre.

I needed to cut out alcohol. Well, maybe I'd just have one day a week, say Saturday, when I could drink what I wanted. We'd see.

As it turned out I gave up alcohol completely. No effort at all.

I'm constantly amazed by my situation, but I intend to continue with what now appears to be a real autobiography.

Had I known what was going to happen after my death I'd have probably killed myself earlier...though perhaps not. If I'd done it earlier, I'd have had less to reminisce about!

Still, I have to say that I'm enjoying my current status. I'm particularly pleased that there seems to be no retribution for transgressions committed 'below'. Is it 'below'? Or is it 'above' or 'somewhere to the side'? Who knows?

In fact, who cares?

I feel satisfied, vindicated, if you like, that I had been particularly sceptical about organised religions' ideas of 'down there'...or 'to the side'!

I wish I could return as a kind of Messiah and tell everyone the truth.

I suppose prophets have been doing that for millennia. Few believe them. Why would they believe me?

Maybe I *will* return as a Messiah. I'll annoy people enough that they'll kill me and then I'll start over again.

But I really don't believe that I *will* return, that I *can* return.

I think this is it.

Chapter Ten   The Next Project

Now, to project number two…

If I'd spoken about it to those people I'd worked with, the suggestion that I might be even remotely capable of killing someone would have been laughed to scorn. My family, had they still existed, would have reacted in the same way, but that was the very reason I'd included it in my list.

I was never an active sort of a chap, never aggressive. I was no 'couch potato' but was never attracted towards participation in team sports, particularly those that involved kicking or carrying a ball, but I was hardly inactive. I walked a lot. In my teenage years I did a lot of what is called 'fell-walking' in the North of England. I spent a lot of time 'Oop North' doing that and doing lots of rock climbing and when I came to Australia I spent many long weekends and annual holidays bush walking, the Watagans, the Daintree, Kakadu, The Blue Mountains, those sorts of places, sometimes with a group but mostly on my own.

I'd thought about it a lot and came to believe that the fact that killing was something I wasn't 'cut out for' was the very reason that I wanted to do it.

I started to think a 'famous' person might not be the ideal target. There were a lot of 'famous' people who deserved to die, some because of their anti-social actions; politicians, 'captains of industry', and journalists would be in this group while there were others who warranted demise on the basis of their crassness. Some film stars, pop singers and 'celebrities' fell into that category. A 'rap' singer would be perfect. *They* all deserved to die, of that there was no question, but they were mostly, if not exclusively, black and I didn't want to harbour any suspicions that my motivation had been in any way racist, because I don't agree with racism. I want to make that clear.

Unfortunately, almost without exception, admirers of such people that I've mentioned above would have been prone to shows of public grief, which would have ensured that the police would take note and concentrate much effort on apprehending the 'guilty' party.

The truth was that I didn't want to be involved in any kind of manhunt. I wanted to do it and then disappear. So what I needed was a person who would not be missed by society in general but whose loss would carry some significance, particularly within a small coterie of friends and associates.

A 'crime boss' was the obvious choice here, but which one? I wanted to settle on someone and settle on them for good; no changes of mind. And yet I knew no criminals, let alone their bosses, and I had no idea of how such people could be contacted.

Meanwhile, I completed my first month in 'The Gym' and I felt one hundred per cent fit. Well, not so much fit as much stronger than when I started. Some of the weights I was using on the machines I'd have had no chance of dealing with at the beginning, in fact, I don't think I could have moved them. I'm exaggerating, of course, but I was really surprised by how much confidence that gave me. I started daydreaming of being challenged physically by, say, a psychopath. 'I'd like to see you try!' I'd say, 'Come on, have a go if you fancy yourself!'

My ideal target would, I supposed be someone who was known for violence, then I'd feel much better about seriously hurting them before I killed them. I supposed it would be a man though I'd have had no qualms about it being a woman. Much more likely to be a man, though.

I can't think of anything relevant to say, so I won't say anything.

What I really need to do is take a break from the autobiography project and think about my current situation, which I find confusing.

Frankly, I think these occasional comments from wherever I am, add little to my tale, so I might give them a rest. If however, I think of something meaningful, I'll revert.

Actually, one of the things I've noticed since my arrival here after the explosion is that I think of meaningful things quite frequently. So you will probably hear from me again. I suspect in the near future.

(I suggest you forget I ever said any of the above. Can't delete it, I'm afraid!)

Chapter Eleven   'Castro' Revisited

I think it only reasonable that I go a little deeper into my *obsession* – it's the only word – with Mando Oliver and specifically, his character 'Castro Mulligan' in the BBC series *Whipsnade*.

Frankly, I was worried. To be this obsessed just wasn't in my nature and yet I had somehow become addicted to the idea of taking on the persona of 'Castro Mulligan'. I was behaving like a teenage girl.

I have had more than my share of women. Well, more than I would have anticipated anyway, mainly after my marriage. Women in the latter part of the Twentieth Century and the early party of the Twenty-first seemed to be readily 'available'. I think this rather pleasant phenomenon had something to do with 'Women's Liberation'. The feeling seemed to be that if men could be promiscuous, then so could, and should, women. I don't think women really wanted that situation but, like my peers, I wasn't going to complain!

As I've said, this nearly all took place after my wife's death, so I had no feelings of guilt about what I was doing. The women I'm talking about seemed overly aggressive. I noticed that this was particularly so at the end of an evening; say at a social gathering after a seminar or a conference or simply in a pub so maybe I was just getting the 'dregs'. Nevertheless, they all seemed very nice to me, albeit with 'baggage'. They all had some, although it was of no real concern because I never had any intention of pursuing relationships. They all seemed very keen to get into bed though and were keen to be, shall we say, 'less than inhibited'?

That seemed to be the ambience of the times.

I knew, despite all this, that I was less than attractive physically and was no great shakes with regard to personality. I found 'small talk', for example, a terrible struggle and anecdotes from my life almost impossible. The truth was, as I freely admit, I'd had a happy but rather uninteresting life.

In my later years I frequently mused about who I'd have preferred to have been. A sportsman? Possibly. A senior politician? Not really. An Army General? Possibly. A famous film star? Maybe. There were other options.

It always came back to the latter idea though…a famous film star.

However, my final selection as you know was not exactly famous.

Let me clarify. As you already know, I'd watched, via DVD, the complete (thus far) British television series called *Whipsnade*. I found it to be a series that held my excited attention without lapse from the beginning of episode one until the final episode and the character that stood out for me, apart from the heroine, was 'Castro Mulligan' a character played by Mando Oliver.

Yes, that was who I wanted to be or at least who I would have liked to have been; Castro Mulligan and yet Castro was really Mando Oliver. It was confusing. Besides, I had seen other TV series that I'd liked and enjoyed watching characters that had 'stood out' for me, yet I'd never experienced the obsession that was with me now.

I began some research into Mando Oliver.

What a strange given name for a man. I looked him up on the computer. His actual name was Mandel. He was the son of Ukrainian Jewish migrants to the U.K. Why on earth did they call him Mandel? It means 'Almond' in German, and I suppose Yiddish too, doesn't it? Who would name their son after a nut? 'Peanut Oliver'? 'Cashew-nut Oliver'? 'Pecan Oliver'? No, I don't think so. Of course, it wouldn't be in English, but would Jewish parents call their son 'Fistashke'? (I looked that up on 'Google Translate', it means 'peanut' in Yiddish.) It was all very strange. And, in any case, there were some pictures of Mr Oliver on the 'Internet' and without the beard I wasn't so sure I wanted to be like him. I'd only seen one other film in which he'd appeared, and I didn't even remember the character he played, so he obviously didn't create an 'impression'.

I had realised by now that I really wanted to be 'Castro Mulligan'. It seems strange that I wanted to become a character of fiction. Was I hankering after transformation into a chimera? Were there any parallels? Perhaps there were.

Young boys, in the time that I myself was a young boy, wanted to be Roy Rogers or 'The Lone Ranger', tough but compassionate cowboys. I don't think anybody wanted to be 'Hopalong' Cassidy. In today's parlance, poor old 'Hoppy' would doubtless be deemed 'uncool'. Ridiculous hat!

Maybe the young men of the Nineteenth Century dreamt of being D'Artagnan or Allan Quatermain or Jean Valjean. Certainly, the rebellious teenage boys of my generation wanted to be Caleb Trask or Jim Stark although James Dean really *was* those people or seemed to be.

I'm searching for a word that describes someone, factual or fictional that someone wants to be, but I can't find it. 'Role model' of course springs to mind but that's not exactly it, is it? I don't mean someone you'd like to be *like*. I mean someone you'd actually like to *be*. I can't seem to get it but there must be a word that covers it. I'll have to invent one. A 'Morphosian' perhaps?

Whipsnade is a sort of huge open-plan zoo in Bedfordshire, England, and the concept was that underneath the zoo was a complex of offices and computer rooms that housed a spy network independent of MI5 and MI6. The main access, though not the only one, was via a small design business located in a village near the zoo's perimeter. The head man of the organisation, which was referred to simply as 'Whipsnade' was this fellow 'Mulligan' and that's who I wanted to look like…to be. There was no doubt that Mr Oliver was a superb actor, but it was his character I admired. I wanted the long, thick black, greying hair - sometimes tied in a 'man-bun' - and beard and the heavy rimmed glasses. I wanted the intense look. I wanted the *sangfroid*, the intellectualism, the calmness and the authority. 'Castro Mulligan' was a man of quiet power in the field of National Security. I wanted to be him, but it would never be. I'm nothing at all like 'Castro Mulligan'. I'd tried to transform myself during my forced period of reclusiveness and failed miserably.

I'd looked up a few more things about Mr Oliver. He was a competent amateur musician - violin - had a good tenor voice and ran a community choir in the Los Angeles suburb of Redondo Beach, where he lived. He collected opium pipes, though I didn't think he used drugs himself. I used to sing in a choir, and I have a good voice. I've never used drugs, except a few times marijuana when I was young (actually quite a lot in Spain when I was twenty-two or thereabouts) but if somebody offered me opium I think I'd smoke it providing there was someone with me who could call an ambulance if necessary. Is that sensible or cowardly? I don't know.

So Mr Oliver was Jewish, which I wasn't, and he was something of a 'Leftist', which I wasn't either. I'd still have liked to have *been* him...or at least 'Castro Mulligan'. But 'Castro Mulligan' *was* Mando Oliver and Mando Oliver *was* 'Castro Mulligan'.

It was strange, I thought, that the boss of the outfit should be called Mulligan because when I was young and lived in England, someone with that name would have been a factory worker or perhaps worked on the roads or the railway. Times change.

Initially, I wasn't sure about 'Castro' either. It's not a name I'd have picked for the character but there was a 'backstory' that I missed at the time. It showed up for me in the book that was written about the series (*Whipsnade – the spies, not the animals!* by Carter Menzies, Daptoe Wilson GBP 14). I duly bought a copy and apparently it was mentioned in 'series one' that 'Mulligan' was the only son of a rather 'left wing' couple who had admired the Cuban revolutionary leader. I was perhaps making a cup of tea when it came up.

Mando Oliver's original name, which he changed by deed poll was Mandel Olshansky. Can't say I blamed him for changing it.

His family probably originated in Olshanske in Ukraine.

It was all 'academic', anyway! I never really dreamt I'd be *like* him, even less *be* him. I began to feel ashamed of myself. I had become a 'TV Tragic'.

In an earlier communication from wherever it is I now am, I said that I found it difficult to relate to my mortal self, or something like that. I might have used the expression 'lack of empathy'. I can't really remember.

However, I can certainly feel connected to that mortal who wanted to become 'Castro Mulligan' because I too certainly feel a 'craving' toward that end. The biggest mistake made by my mortal self in this regard was to confuse the actor Mondo Oliver with the character.

Castro Mulligan was the character, and it was he that I wanted to be.

I think this might be achievable but as yet, I don't know how. Perhaps in the final 'Phase' this will become a possibility. I hope so.

Chapter Twelve   I Research the Sydney Marathon

The first Sydney Marathon came along just after I'd started my training or at least after I'd got about six weeks into it. So I thought I should be an observer even though I wasn't going to run. Get a feel for it, you know.

As it happened, this move on my part was fortuitous because it supplied me with the absolutely perfect target for my second project and it also provided me with the means of *entrapping* my target. (More of this later.)

I had decided to move into town for three nights, which would give me one day before the race and one day after it. No hurry; I didn't want that.

On the day of the race, I got up early at the hotel in which I was staying. I won't mention the name of the hotel, which is actually a 'payback'. The truth is, I don't want to give the hotel any publicity and the reason for that is that the hotel, supposedly one of the best in Sydney was overpriced and, in my opinion, the staff were rude...or should that be *was* rude?

Anyway, I got up early, had a quick breakfast from the admittedly excellent buffet and was down to Bradfield Park at Milsons Point in time for the start.

The Harbour Bridge was closed to traffic, but it was interesting to see how the different categories went off. I think this is how it went. The wheelchair lot went off first and then, five minutes later, the 'elites' and so on down the line until the last group, which were the least experienced and the one I'd join next year, or maybe the year after. I jogged back over the Bridge using the narrow walkway on the Eastern side and then used the stairs down to the Quay and up to the Park where I sat down on the grass and waited for the leaders. I didn't have to wait long; in fact, I only just got there in time.

The leaders were all black, three of them and they all looked as though they'd benefit from a large plate of steak and chips. After them came the local elite Aussie guys although a few singlets emblazoned with stars and stripes and union jacks and one French '*tricolour*' were interspersed.

Following them came the 'no-hopers' and the 'wankers' and it was interesting for me to evaluate many of them by running style, clear in the knowledge that they had totally misjudged their programme and that they had far outpaced themselves in the very early part of the race. This makes me sound like an expert after only six weeks, which is not my intention, but even a complete novice learns a lot about style quite quickly. Many of those early leaders would finish with a very high number against their names or more likely would not finish at all. On the other hand, there were those in this early group whose running styles were like works of art; their grace and elegance bringing tears to my eyes, I don't mind admitting. I should have brought a pen and notepad with me to record the runners whom I'd have wagered would achieve a top ten spot. I tried to remember those that I'd fancied but I wasn't successful, and I forgot them all!

I continued to watch the runners until I thought the last one had passed…maybe there were more to come, I'm not sure, but then I walked over to the 'Café in the Park' and ordered a coffee and a muffin, after which I walked back down Macquarie Street to the Opera House and the finish.

The winner was a black guy from Kenya and the second guy was Ethiopian but the third to the tenth were all white, mainly Aussies but there were two Poms plus a Yank and a German before the next black guy who wasn't Kenyan but I can't remember where he was from. Mozambique? Maybe. Where did the German come from? I don't remember seeing him in the Park. Maybe he just joined in for the last kilometre. I doubt it! But it's been done before, at an early Olympics I believe.

Anyway, I'd enjoyed the experience and looked forward to being a part of 'the action' next year, although probably the year after. I spent the rest of the morning and most of the afternoon walking around Sydney. I went to the Art Gallery and the Museum; both worth a visit, then back to the hotel for a little 'shuteye' before dinner.

I quite enjoy a sleep in the afternoon. I wake up after about an hour and lie daydreaming for another one which usually brings the time up to about five-thirty, at which time, I get up, have a wash and have my first drink prior to dinner between six-thirty and seven.

Being in a hotel my programme became more leisurely. After waking, I 'raided the mini-bar' for a miniature whisky and followed that with a small bottle of rather nice Shiraz which I enjoyed while watching the Evening News on the television.

Afterwards, I had a quick shower and then went downstairs for dinner.

Chapter Thirteen   Office 'Politics' and Insecurities

It was around that time that I went through the most severe period of self-doubt and insecurity since retirement. Funnily enough, I'm not a self-assured person though many would find that hard to believe. It was my persona as a salesman that was responsible for that. I was actually a very good salesman and in a perverse way it was my insecurity that gave to me the impression of being confident. My insecurity made me seem empathetic toward my clients, my potential and existing customers.

Initially, I wrote things down, things about each of my 'targets', things like birthdays, wife's name, number of children, their car, if they liked dogs, those sorts of things, but after a while I had no need for my 'little black book' because I found I could easily remember everything. I had a very good memory at the time, not so good now but that's to be expected, I suppose.

That was my image, how I 'came across'; caring, empathetic, interested, consoling even from time to time. I became their friend even though I couldn't abide some of the bastards. And I got sales and sales meant commissions. I always worked on commission and when they tried to change the system, my terms of employment, to a salaried position and then, under further protest, to a base salary and a much lower commission, I refused to accept it. I didn't threaten to resign and as it turned out, I didn't have to. My father, the 'chain store' executive, always told me that if I ever found myself in the position of having 'the goods' - as he put it - on anybody but particularly my boss, then the trick was simply to make sure that they knew that *you* knew. No need to threaten 'disclosure unless something is done for my benefit'. That was called blackmail and the police don't like blackmailers. You just had to let them know that *you* knew and the benefits would arrive. It intrigues me now that my 'straight-laced' father told me this.

Unfortunately, I knew nothing of an incriminating nature about anybody.

My boss at the time was not a bad bloke. He'd just been transferred from Canada, although he was French by birth. Jean-Marc Monet was his name, and he was a distant relative of the artist, or said he was! The arch prick Mike Brotchie, my previous boss - more of him later - had been transferred to Head Office in the States.

One evening shortly after Jean-Marc's arrival I was working late. Nobody was aware of my presence since I'd travelled into work by cab and intended to go home on the train. My car was at the panel beaters for a minor repair so there was no evidence of my presence at the office. There were no cars in the car park other than Jean-Marc's and that of one of the 'office girls'. The office closed at five p.m. and it was now six forty-five. I could understand Jean-Marc's car being there, bosses always work late, but why had Brenda from 'Accounts' left her car behind when she'd gone home? Perhaps it wouldn't start or perhaps she'd gone to the local pub for a quick drink with colleagues after work.

I walked out to the lobby and saw no one. In fact, there didn't seem to be a light on in the offices other than that on my desk in the Sales Office. I went downstairs and again there were no lights on but then I saw a light under the door of the records room. I had the habit of slipping out of my shoes in the office - I'm not comfortable in business shoes - so, *definitely* without evil intent - I walked, inevitably quietly, towards the records room, meaning to switch off the light which plainly had been left burning, perhaps by a careless clerk.

I opened the door and secured my terms of employment in Comptex!

There on the floor was Jean-Marc, Brenda from 'Accounts' and another rather large-breasted girl who was unknown to me. All were stark naked. The stunned facial expressions were a joy to behold.

I closed the door quietly and went home.

Well, the management (*surprise, surprise!*) gave in, my 'commission-only' deal was continued, and I celebrated by doubling sales in my final year, which gave me one Hell of a salary for the period. Of course, I knew that sales would be good that year, although naturally I'd put in a pessimistic budget forecast. The whole exercise cost the company a 'bomb' but I got them the sales so they had to pay me.

Then I retired. It was two years after my wife died.

It was a strange feeling, being alone and I was completely in that state, with no wife, no kids, no grandkids, and no living relatives, and it was then that my insecurity came back.

Now, allow me to tell you a little more about myself, particularly with regard to my physical appearance. I think it's relevant.

I was rather white of skin, I didn't tan easily, in fact, I reddened and when, after a day or two, the redness disappeared I reverted to the original white. I'd sought medical solutions to this 'problem' but was assured, by doctors, that there was no cure.

'So,' I'd thought, 'be it'.

In addition, I had sandy hair.

My mother and my grandmother used to tell me how beautiful my hair was. They were kind and loving people.

In addition, I had freckles and mum and grandma told me how attractive that was.

And I had green eyes. My female forebears liked them too. Or said they did.

However, I soon found out that having white, freckly skin and sandy hair were not seen as advantages in the sexual stakes.

The green eyes appealed to some girls.

Now to physique.

I was quite tall at one hundred and eighty-seven centimetres. That's about six foot one but I was very 'skinny' and my empathetic persona had encouraged a slight bending from the waist and a hunching of the shoulders a posture that gave the impression of my being 'concerned', which had proved useful in my selling career.

Chapter Fourteen   A Relationship Endangered

Now, I've probably given the impression that I was essentially a loner. This is far from the truth. In fact, people would be quite surprised when I say - which reminds me of the limerick about The Dowager Countess of Bray (the second line goes, "You'll be quite surprised when I say,") - that after my wife died, I gained a girlfriend. Without implying any disrespect, I suppose the first part of that word should be written between quotation marks because she - her name was Anita - was sixty-two years old and she'd been married and had a daughter who lived with her. Anita's first and only pregnancy occurred when she was forty-two years old and not surprisingly, risk was anticipated. Yet it was a perfect birth and the child, a girl, perfectly formed, was quite beautiful. However, as she grew and thrived it became clear that there were problems. At first, I heard later, these were greeted with denials, everything had gone so well, but eventually the truth was accepted and as is often the case, the husband found himself unable to accept reality and left.

The mentally retarded though physically beautiful daughter still lived with Anita and fortunately was largely self-sufficient, spending much of her time painting, mainly in acrylics. She'd done some works in oils and she'd even stretched to watercolours although the latter was not her favourite medium.

Surprisingly, well, surprisingly to me although Anita didn't agree, she painted extremely competently, far better than I could ever have managed but she was loath to exhibit or to offer anything for sale. She - Annette was her name - was fully aware of her disabilities and refused to let her 'defects' influence any success that might have been due. She thought they *would*. I believed that was wrong and said so, but Anita disagreed and supported her daughter's attitude. It annoyed the Hell out of me.

Annette's paintings would have been, I suppose, classed as 'naive' or 'primitive'. Whenever I saw her stuff, I immediately thought of Lowry, but she was different. In my humble opinion, she was twice the painter that Lowry had been and I was a great fan of *his* works. I'd visited the *Lowry Museum* in Salford, England and I'd happily go there again. But Annette had something that Lowry never had. Well, you could argue that he *did* have it but Annette had more. I thought the correct word, the correct quality, would be 'pathos'. She seemed to be able to paint a scene with no human or animal figures and give you a feeling of sadness. Her faces - though she rarely used faces - made you want to cry. In fact, she once told me that she avoided faces because they actually *did* make her cry as she painted them. Her portraits were rare and far from photographic but absolutely superb and there could never have been any confusion regarding the subject but, again in my opinion, she added, consciously or unconsciously, I don't know, something of the character of her subjects that would never have appeared in a photograph. She spent ages, up to a year, on each painting and never less than four months, although she often had three or four paintings 'on the go' at any one time.

She kept to her room mainly, yet I had several quite complex conversations with her. Yes, incredibly complex. It was, well, shocking.

In my opinion, she was the best painter in Australia, and it was a crying shame she wouldn't exhibit. I'd been talking to her about it. I'd told her that I'd be happy to be a sort of Marketing Manager for her. I think she could see the points I was making but she still, stubbornly refused to show anything she'd produced. I suppose, in a way, she was an 'idiot savant'.

I used to watch Annette when she took her bath. She always bathed when Anita was cooking dinner, so Anita was occupied, and I used to say I was going to 'kill some time' by doing a bit of reading or doing some reports. I was still working at the time although in my final year of employment. I'd do that whilst lying on the bed, Anita's bed. Actually, this was for the most part true. I did lie on the bed, and I did read but now and again I'd watch Annette in the bath. She always left the door ajar - she was slightly claustrophobic - I think I watched her because I felt protective towards her.

There was a habit Annette had of totally submerging herself in the water. She'd lie back and let herself sink until her body, including her head, was submerged. Then she'd hold her breath and stay submerged for quite a long time, a frighteningly long time. Sometimes, she'd lie on her front with her head submerged. I thought nothing much of it.

Yes, I really *had* thought nothing much of it, but I'd become more and more frustrated by her attitude towards her paintings. It was such a waste, and I became obsessed with changing her mind on the matter. This was difficult or, to be realistic, impossible. Strangely, the more I considered the problem, the more I saw different aspects and it dawned on me that because of the high quality of her works, the idea of keeping them from the general population was in so many ways selfish, even iniquitous. Why should the population at large be barred from seeing these wonderful paintings? I thought about it a great deal before I made my decision.

One evening, it was a Wednesday, I remember, Anita was downstairs in the kitchen creating a quite complex French dish. She was an excellent cook. I was upstairs on the bed and Annette was in the bath. I went quietly to the bathroom door as I'd done many times before. Annette was lying quite still. She was smiling, remembering some happy event I supposed or perhaps seeing clearly the next 'move' in her latest painting, a revelation perhaps.

Suddenly she returned from her reverie and looking triumphant, she turned over and submerged herself face downwards in the bathwater. I waited a few seconds and then moved quietly to the side of the bath. With the heels of my hands, I pressed firmly on the middle of Annette's back and then moved up to her shoulders. I remember thinking how beautiful her skin was. It was a creamy colour and smooth as silk but softer than that material, much softer. She made initial resistance, but her movements were more in surprise than fear and far less strenuous than I'd expected. I felt a stirring in my lower body. Was that sexual or was it just the excitement in what I was doing? I think the latter. Air bubbled up from around her beautiful head and I believe she anticipated rising from the water and taking a breath of air. My hands and rigid arm muscles rendered this impossible, and she must have inhaled bathwater. She went limp…quite suddenly.

I released the pressure on Annette's shoulders and she stayed stable, submerged as before in the water. I guessed that the intake of water and the lack of air in her lungs would have radically changed her buoyancy. I dried my hands and returned to the bedroom. Very soon afterwards, I heard Anita's call to dinner.

All this had pre-dated my 'bucket' short-list of three commitments so it didn't count. Someone else would need to die.

Now, I've told you, in the previous chapter about something I'm not proud of. Actually, I'm rather ashamed of it and were it not for my current knowledge, as the writer of this autobiography, of lack of both judgment and punishment in the after-life, I wouldn't have revealed this at all.

I've frequently thought about what I did to Annette.

I believed that what I'd done was justified. Anyone who was interested in art should have the opportunity to see, or read, or hear the masterpieces of human endeavour.

I'm sure that's right.

At the same time, Annette's life itself was of little value, to her or indeed to anybody. She was mentally retarded, not radically but 'to some extent'. I don't want to appear a 'eugenicist' here but I'm sure most people will understand the point I'm making.

Her mother had wasted years of her life caring for her. Her mother's marriage had broken up because of her.

Anita deserved some recompense and that would have been provided by the systematic sale of her daughter's paintings.

I wanted nothing for myself.

What I had done had been accomplished in the spirit of altruism.

I repeat: I wanted nothing for myself.

Just as an aside, and being reminded by mention of the 'Dowager Countess', I rather like limericks. The 'original' ones were supposedly written by Edward Lear or at least, he was reputed to have popularised the form. However, in my opinion, Lear's limericks were rather poor, depending as he did, on the repetition of the first line or elements thereof in the final line.

Here's an example:

'There was an old person from Ems
Who casually fell in the Thames

And when he was found
They said he had drowned
That unfortunate person from Ems'

Not very good is it?

Well, later limericks, whilst depending to some great extent on vulgarity are up there with Thomas Grey's 'Elegy in a Country Churchyard' or Keats's 'To Autumn', in my opinion at least.

The secret of a good limerick is surely the surprise in the final line but even this is improved by elements of improbability, like the 'Dowager Countess of Bray', who 'despite her high station and fine education' 'She always spelt 'cunt' with a 'k'!'

Here's one that I particularly like:

'There was an old man from Bengal
Who had a mathematical ball
Three times the weight into pi minus eight
Was the twenty-third root of fuck-all'

I'm digressing again; I suppose most people will assume so and in many ways they're right. However, in this case, there is some justification for the digression because I see the limerick as...I'm not sure of the correct word, although I've forgotten it rather than never known it...I'll try to remember it and let you know if I do, by the end of this autobiography. What I'm trying to say is that the limerick with its four-line form - the good ones, at least - is a kind of representation of my life. The first line is always the introduction i.e. 'me', the second is the ambition i.e. to run a marathon, to kill somebody etc., the third is the anticipation, for example, I begin running the marathon, and the fourth is how it turns out. There is always optimism in the form, but the final line can indicate success or failure, acclaim, or ridicule. With me, my fourth line seems to be ridicule lately although my experience with Monsieur Monet and Brenda from Accounts had certainly been 'acclaim'. My 'fourth line' with the Sydney Marathon and the treatment of my target for assassination would turn out quite the reverse, as you shall see. I just wish I could remember the word.

I don't think there was a sexual component in my watching Annette in the bath. Maybe there was but if so, I didn't recognise it.

What is the point of this self-deceit, this blatant lie? Yes, actually I do recognise it and the admission *for the first time* is having a cleansing effect on me.

I have nothing now to lose, no embarrassment, no humiliation, and, more importantly, no criminal charges, which would have brought their own humiliation.

I can admit, that when watching Annette in the bath I had experienced erections. This was especially so when she lifted her upper body from the bath water and her glistening breasts sort of wobbled. 'Tremored' might be a better word.

I've become unsure of my motives in killing Annette. My current environment has led to a stronger quest for honesty.

In reality, what I had accomplished as my mortal self was probably the greatest incidence of rationalisation in the whole of my life!

By any morality, by any creed or religion, what I had done was an anathema. To kill, in any circumstance, was against human nature, wasn't it?

Well, no, there were certain cases where it was justified, 'capital punishment' in extreme circumstances was one of them. Euthanasia - an unfortunate euphemism - in circumstances where severe pain was present or where the 'victim' had pleaded for its use, was another.

But neither had been the case in Annette's situation. My actions had been altruistic...at least I had thought them to be so, but ultimately the action had been for my own selfish mortal ends.

I deserved punishment. I expected it yet, thankfully, such an outcome was not about to arrive.

The word I was looking for, by the way, was 'allegory'...I think.

(I find it 'passing strange' that notwithstanding I am dead and can therefore not worry about resulting opprobrium I can happily admit, in my 'autobiography', to murder and yet am reluctant to admit to sexual arousal.)

Chapter Fifteen   A Price Paid

Well, the aftermath of the bathroom incident was devastating, although not initially. Anita had called Annette to come down, but she was always late and even when she was on time, she would sit staring at her meal until it was barely lukewarm. Then she'd start eating. It was one of those concessions that Anita made for her daughter. It always annoyed me although I never made comment.

After we'd eaten the superb main course, Anita said, "I'd better go up and check".

"She'll be fine", I said. There was a shake in my voice, though Anita hadn't noticed it. She left her chair and went upstairs.

I felt my heart thumping against my ribcage. I was shaking.

There was a pause and then a scream.

Anita was hysterical and I took on the role of distraught partner, calling an ambulance and the police. I was questioned, of course but my obvious agitation, my concern for Annette and the lack of marks on the body ensured that my role as suspect was quickly lost and the coroner was convinced that death had been either accidental or possibly - although it was never mentioned in the report - suicide. I've since learnt that the most efficient way to drown somebody in a bath is to grab the ankles and raise the legs. They slide down under the water and are rendered helpless. Still, I don't suppose I'll have the occasion to check that out.

There was a funeral, a small one, with few guests but quite nicely officiated by a member of the undertaker's staff - Anita was not religious - and in due course everything returned to normal.

Anita maintained her equilibrium despite the tragedy. Her love for her daughter had been total and unconditional though I felt that she failed to fully appreciate her loss or seemed to.

Then I made a mistake.

Of course, I was going to try to convince Anita to release the paintings for, at least, exhibition but how best could I persuade her that the quality of the artworks strongly justified such action?

I decided that I would 'borrow' one of the portraits.

I settled on a wonderfully clever portrait of a female Member of Parliament. The subject was of aboriginal heritage, so 'female' and 'aboriginal' with an unknown but clearly brilliant artist, what could possibly go wrong? Annette's paintings would become highly prized. I knew it.

Annette never signed her work. She had no need since she refused to exhibit or put anything up for sale. So how should I handle the provenance?

I thought about this for a long time and concluded that if I used Annette's imprimatur there would have been problems, or at least the best result might not be attained. It would be better for the prices if a new painting could be released or 'produced' at irregular intervals. If it was known that the artist had been discovered *post-mortem* then surely it would have been expected that the complete works would be released in one fell swoop, thus probably adversely affecting the values. Paintings should be released, ideally, in chronological sequence, because the 'Art World' loves to observe the changes, the 'growth' that occurs during an artist's lifetime.

There was a solution.

I took a fine brush, and some white acrylic and signed my name on the bottom right-hand corner. Then I entered the painting into Australia's best-known art prize, The Archibald Portrait Prize.

Once the win was achieved, as I knew it would be, Anita would see that my *modus operandi* had been correct. She would understand that although the fame would be mine, the financial gain would be hers - I'd make sure all monies for sales would go directly to her - and I'd hoped that in time that would amount to millions of dollars. In addition, she would understand that her beloved daughter's refusal to sell or even exhibit the paintings under her own name would be honoured.

Weeks passed until I got the news.

The painting had been rejected for the 'final cut' and had not even been selected for the Salon des Refuses at the S.H. Erwin Gallery. To say I was shattered would have been an understatement. I couldn't bring myself to collect 'my' work. I would wait until I'd calmed down and then collect with unconcerned nonchalance. Unfortunately, my wait for calmness took rather too long for the Art Gallery of New South Wales and a telephone call was made, which Anita took.

To say 'the shit hit the fan' would be an understatement.

Our relationship was over and no amount of argument, made in an effort to justify my actions, was accepted. Though my involvement in Annette's death remained undetected.

Looking back, it seems that my regrets concerned the break in my relationship with Anita, rather than with my deceit.

I feel now that I should have been ashamed of my actions - the killing and the forgery - but I don't recall that being the case.

Where I am, wherever I am now, there is no shame, no regret, no hurtful self-blame yet I feel I should have felt something. Perhaps, at the time, I did feel some shame. That would have been natural but now, I don't remember feeling anything.

Chapter Sixteen   A Relationship Begun and Ended

There's an expression, which most likely originated in the African-American milieu that goes, 'When you're hot, you're hot!'. A more civilised expression of this sentiment might be, 'Success breeds success'. Either way, I agree that it's true.

When I was at the height of my relationship with Anita I noticed that I was being 'targeted' by numerous other women. It was as though I was emitting some aura of sexuality that hitherto had been hidden, or more likely had not existed. It was at that time I had been approached by Deirdre.

Deirdre was an enigma. I was attracted to her in a weakly physical - she was sexually unattractive - but strongly intellectual way. She was patently more intelligent than me but the time for such a liaison was not propitious, my involvement with Anita was all-consuming.

My relationship with Deirdre was not pursued.

I saw nothing more of Deirdre until several weeks after my split with Anita.

As I've said, Deidre was sexually unattractive. What I meant was the poor girl was positively ugly. She had thin, mousy hair, her eyes were small and close set, her teeth were uneven and her jaw line was much pronounced. She wore no make-up.

Her figure was acceptable though her hips were large and seemed to extend too far down her thighs.

Despite all this, I found her company a delight. She was a university professor of languages and as well as being fluent in French, German and Russian was extremely well read. Her politics were somewhat to the left of mine, but she respected my opinions and was careful to avoid confrontations on political subjects.

I met up with Deirdre again quite by chance, after my break-up with Anita, and we began 'seeing' each other.

My relationship with Deirdre was exclusively on an intellectual level. Generally, she spoke, and I was happy to listen. But Deirdre's attraction to me was surprisingly otherwise.

Not to put too fine a point on it, she wanted to go to bed with me.

'Well', I thought, 'so be it. What will be, will be'. After various delaying tactics over several weeks, we reserved a table at a very expensive restaurant near Deirdre's apartment prior to what was plainly going to be the culmination of her desire.

We talked over the various excellent courses and superb wine at great length. Deirdre introduced the works of Dostoevsky as subject matter, which was fortunate for me since I'd read three of that author's major works and was therefore able to contribute. We'd covered *Crime and Punishment* and were discussing *The Idiot* when the desserts were finished and coffee was contemplated. Deirdre immediately vetoed the coffee idea; I paid the bill and we left.

And then disaster.

Deirdre's body was quite attractive and lying down her hips didn't seem so pronounced. Her breasts were firm and well-rounded and her vulva, whilst singular - to use the word in its archaic sense - was not uninviting.

The disaster I've referred to came in the form of my not being able to raise an erection.

Deirdre was 'understanding'. She told me not to worry and held me close. We slept.

In the morning she made fresh advances but again I was unable to perform.

We parted on good terms after a hearty breakfast, but I never saw Deirdre again. I'd been 'dumped'.

I learnt later from a neighbour of hers that she had gone 'overseas'. To the question, 'Do you know where?' I got the reply, 'No idea, mate. Europe somewhere, I think'. Not very helpful and I didn't really believe him, although what would I have been able to do had I known the exact location?

A lesson learnt, a lesson I deserved perhaps but my condition worried me.

In truth, the whole episode depressed me. Masturbation was not effective, so a brothel was tried. The prostitute was incredibly beautiful. She was many years younger than me and tried everything. I won't elaborate. She did her best, but the result was the same. Nothing.

At this point in my existence I decided that my sex life was over.

Chapter Seventeen   Past Success then Disabuse

Up until then - my relationships with Anita and Deirdre - my life had been 'very ordinary', that's the only way to describe it. I suppose I could say 'very boring', but I don't think that would have been quite accurate. Married life, dinner parties, kids, coaching or managing football teams, socialising with the netball 'crowd', going on camping holidays, trying to understand teenagers etc.... all the usual stuff.

Yes, there *had* been interesting occurrences. After all, I had spent a great deal of my life in 'sales' in the most vibrant industry around at the time and the 'attendant virtues' were legion. We worked, or perhaps I should say 'we *were* worked' extremely hard but (Oh Boy!) did we get paid well if we were successful!

My biggest earning years came in my early fifties. I was still working for Comptex, an American company and didn't you know it? The boss was a Yank import, Mike Brotchie, who was an absolute 'arsehole' and extremely seriously 'vertically challenged'. He regarded himself as God's gift to 'industry' and made our lives Hell. His management techniques revolved around unfair criticism and threats of dismissal. Since we all knew how good a wicket we were on regarding work effort and monetary reward, we put up with the peccadillos of Mr Brotchie, or 'Stumpy' as we called him, behind his back, of course. Brotchie's wife, Eileen, was something else, taller than her husband, darker complexion, delightful company and very, very sexy.

I went to bed with Eileen Brotchie once. I believed for some time that the seducing had been mine though I was later disillusioned. After this single incident I had felt myself to be in love with Eileen and was planning how the upcoming change of relationship could be transmitted to my wife and children with the least possible hurt when I received a call from her.

I was in the car on my way home, two days later, when the call came through and the gist of it was that Eileen's husband had become suspicious and that 'for the sake of my career' we should immediately call the affair off. I was led to believe that Mike Brotchie was a violent man who would not hesitate to carry out severe physical abuse of his wife should the affair be confirmed. I protested, I would protect my lover, 'my job meant nothing', we would be 'together forever'.

But Eileen was adamant. I wept, but my tears were followed by reality and reality was followed by relief. I stopped at the 'bottle shop' on the way home and bought a bottle of vintage champagne.

My marriage was safe, but Brotchie seemed to be singling me out for his aggression over the next couple of weeks. After a while his aggression abated, and he left me alone for a while. I thought at the time he had discovered his wife's infidelity and he was taking out his anger on me. Afterwards, I thought I'd simply been paranoid and the master to servant approach by Brotchie had been coincidence rather than revenge.

Sometime later, I was at a computer industry conference at which there were several sales people, all male, who had worked at Comptex or been closely associated with it in various countries. I knew most of the guys and towards the end of the evening there remained a hard core of drinkers who had known Mike Brotchie, who was now tormenting the sales staff at Comptex, San Francisco.

We had congregated around a vacant table; stories were exchanged and memories reminisced upon. One of the group was a little more drunk and a little more voluble than the rest of us and when Brotchie's name came up he freely admitted having bedded 'Stumpy's' wife. This admission was greeted with uproarious laughter, but the laughter was tinged, I thought, with embarrassment. The result of the unexpected admission was an avalanche of similar admissions. Of the eight guys around the table, six admitted to having had a brief affair with Eileen. I was the last and I suppose because of that and my general aura of being a 'non-player' I was at first not believed but then Tom Klemstein, the lone Yank in the throng asked what, if anything, did I notice about Eileen Brotchie's body. I remember blushing quite violently but then said, "Her nipples," and my claim was immediately accepted. I was one of 'The Boys'.

The discussion continued and it seemed that liaisons had occurred in Sydney, London, Geneva, Dallas, Washington and Dublin; all places where Brotchie had been in charge of the office and all at times coinciding with his absence at Head Office in Houston, Texas.

It was Frank Hardrey who dropped the bombshell. When the laughter of incredulity had died down, he said, "I firmly believe that Brotchie was in the next room or somewhere, watching". Hardrey's comment was greeted with silence, but a silence tinged with an air of consideration.

"Well, I don't believe that", said somebody, - I think it was Eric Somerville - "because I dropped him off at the airport and stayed with him until he went through Customs."

So Frank asked, "Did anyone ever pick him up when he came back?"

Nobody volunteered a 'Yes.'

"And did anybody avoid getting picked on by the prick after what happened?"

Again a positive response was not forthcoming.

"And was Eileen's excuse for ending the relationship, concern for each of our careers? And did anybody notice," continued Hardrey, "that the lovely Eileen was very specific about positioning on the bed?"

Many were the responses to *that* question, all along the lines of, "Now you come to mention it" or "Yes, I thought it a bit strange" Or simply, "Fucking Hell!"

One lives and one learns…usually too late. Although I've since learnt that Mike Brotchie died at fifty-eight of a brain tumour.

Served the bastard right.

I was always something of an innocent - naïve would probably be a better descriptor – when it came to sex. At least, that was the case in my teens.

I was in my last year at school and was certainly less 'knowing' about sexual matters than my friends.

As an example, I couldn't quite understand the mechanics of the sexual act. It seemed to me that penetration of one's partner would best be achieved in the standing position. The penis in its erect state was vertical and the vagina was similarly angled. Copulation, I reasoned, would involve a bending of the knees in order to initiate insertion and the intercourse itself would involve a constant bending and straightening of the knees. This would surely involve the head moving up and down too so that the eyes might be looking into one's partner's eyes (assuming similar height) at the zenith of the upstroke and at the neck at the nadir of the downstroke. It didn't seem right, somehow but I was unable to conceive of an alternative. My conclusions would certainly have made horizontal intercourse difficult if not impossible.

My first 'experience' corrected this hypothesis when I discovered that a repeated hip thrust was all that was necessary. This is simply a preamble to what follows.

This was something I'd been putting off until I got the hang of things. I didn't want to endanger the experience. This time I was going for my first sexual experience. I remembered it well; I remembered the feeling, the silkiness, the warmth around my member, or more than warmth; heat, because it was winter and the air was cold. We were in a wood and she, I can't remember her name - Janet? - No! - Maureen, I think - had her back to a tree. It slipped in easily. I can remember that.

Here we go.

Silky smooth, hot, burning even. I am surprised how the penetration is achieved. As I've said, I'd imagined that there would need to be some flexing of the knee joints but find that by pushing my arse in and out, I seem to convert horizontal motion into vertical. Of course, it's the slightly backward angle of the vagina coupled with the lubrication, which causes it, but I hadn't worked that out yet.

And then panic!

I might get her pregnant and have to marry her. I pull out as I orgasm and that which I have produced flies through the frozen air and lands in the grass two metres away, or it seems that far at least. I'm proud of my potency and say so. She laughs, with me…or *at* me? I'm not sure.

I feel proud.

We laugh.

She is standing with her back against a tree. Hot, silky smooth, it flies…over and over and over.

I think I might have chosen a better incident although one always remembers one's first time. It has significance.

Now it will be repeated until I choose to stop it.

Chapter Eighteen   A Humiliation that Turns Out Well

After all that sexual digression, I'll get back to my first contact with the Sydney Marathon.

After a sleep in my hotel room, I had a drink, watched some television, then, I thought I might eat in the hotel restaurant, which looked O.K.

So I went down to the lobby and decided I might splash out a bit and have a drink first at the hotel bar. I don't like doing that so much normally because they charge obscene amounts for a drink…but what the Hell? It was a pretty rare occasion.

The bar at the hotel was outside the restaurant and was quite a big room with a lot of low tables and a central bar shaped like an elongated doughnut with shelves of drinks under the counter and the barmen in the middle. I sat on a stool up at the bar and ordered a drink. Just a beer.

The room was quite crowded, which surprised me because it was early, but I supposed the crowd had all just left work and were having a drink before going home. Then I realised that it was the weekend so the crowd were probably warming up for the theatre or something. It was all rather new to me. The experience, I mean. There was one spare stool to my right and two to my left. I was looking to my right. Actually, I was looking at a very attractive young woman sitting at the far end of the bar with an older man; probably her boss but maybe not, so I was surprised to find when I turned back to my left that the seat next to me had become occupied by a rather large and certainly very fit-looking man. His complexion was on the swarthy side and his hair looked well groomed, as though he'd just come from the barbers.

The guy looked at me and said, "G'day!". I returned his greeting and then he asked how my day had been. I told him about my ambition to run the marathon next year or the year after and how I had spent the day familiarising myself with the procedures. He said, "Right." but didn't show a great deal of interest. I like meeting new people, especially those who come into my life quite by chance, so I decided to develop the conversation.

"I'm retired," I said, "but you're obviously not. So what kind of business are you in?"

"My business," he replied, and my first reaction was that he was telling me that he ran his own small business. I was just about to ask, "And what business is that?" but in retrospect, I'm rather glad I didn't because I had suddenly realised that what he was really saying was, "Mind your own business!"

Anyway, after the initial embarrassment, I thought no more about it because the next thing I saw was that a friend of his had joined him and they had greeted each other with much embracing and backslapping. This seems to be the fashion nowadays.

I returned to reverie, turning away.

Then I overheard my neighbour saying to his friend, something like, "…this prick next to me…what business…and I said, 'my fucking business'…think he…message!" There followed roars of laughter. I paid my bill and left.

I got a table in the restaurant, right at the back where the door to the kitchen was. That was fine. It didn't worry me in the slightest. I ordered a half bottle of wine and studied the menu. When I'd made up my mind on a starter and a main I looked up for the waiter. There were two and my one was taking the order from a table of six a few tables away from me. While I waited I looked towards the entrance and saw my neighbour from the bar come in with his friend. They were shown to a table on the opposite side of the restaurant from mine and nearer the front. I thought the guy I'd spoken to had recognised me as he looked my way and I half smiled in acknowledgement, but he made no response so plainly he didn't.

I thought I knew the chap now but couldn't figure out from where, but he seemed somehow familiar. A politician? A film or TV actor? I decided I might ask the Concierge who seemed a friendly sort of a cove.

The meal, though expensive, was very good and I even stretched to a dessert, which seemed to consist mainly of liquid chocolate surrounded by chocolate cake. Excellent! And why should I have continued with my lifetime habit of frugality? I had plenty of money, I didn't owe anything, there was just me and if my plans worked out, I wouldn't have to spend it all before I went. Perhaps, I thought, I *should* spend it all. Maybe what I'd planned would *cost* all I had. All would be revealed!

I paid the bill, added a generous tip, left the restaurant and headed out to the lobby and the Concierge, who greeted me like a long-lost friend. I suppose that's what they're trained to do.

"Can I assist you, sir?" asked the Concierge.

"Maybe you can, maybe you can't", I replied.

"Let's see, sir, shall we?" he smiled.

"Well, in the restaurant there're two blokes. They're at the third table along the wall at the right-hand side. I'm sure I recognise the bigger of the two, the one with the black hair combed straight back. It's driving me mad. Would you know who he is? His mate too if you know."

"Give me two seconds," said the Concierge and walked quickly towards the restaurant, into which he disappeared.

Almost immediately, he returned and said, "You picked a good'un!"

I asked, "How so?"

And he said, "The big guy's Stefano Collins, not sure about his mate, never seen him before but probably a…shall we say, 'business colleague'?"

I said, "Still none the wiser. What's he do?"

"You've probably seen his picture in the paper. Runs most of the drugs and girls in The Cross. Not a *'nice'* chap. Not nice at all. Wouldn't want to cross him. Many have tried, few have succeeded, with or without hands, or actually 'fingers', if you get my drift. Brutal, he is. No prisoners."

"Right. Suppose he looks the part."

"Wouldn't think he bats for the other team, would you?"

I had to think about that, and then I said, "Well he certainly looks like he could be a crook."

"You never heard that expression?"

"Batting for the other team?"

"Yes."

"No, I haven't."

"He's…" he leered, "he likes men."

"You mean he's a homosexual?"

"That's about it! That bar through there is a bit of a gay hangout. He comes in here from time to time. Often leaves with somebody he didn't come in with. Big tipper, but."

"Well, you live and learn."

"You do, sir, you do! Anything else I can help you with?"

"Er, no. No thanks, not at the moment. I'm off for an early night."

"Good night, sir!"

I pressed the lift button and the door opened immediately. The lift was empty. I stepped inside and pressed my floor button. As the lift rose, I smiled and said, "Thank you, God! Thank you!"

I had found my target for the second thing. I punched the air.

On reflection, here was a case where embarrassment became a benefit. I really don't think - no, I'm sure of it - that I'd have followed up on Stefano 'Steve' Collins had he not made me look a fool. I'd never have approached the Concierge regarding his details.

In a way, this can be explained by the Oriental concept of Yin and Yang, something good compensating for something bad, although I'm not absolutely sure that the actual concept of that philosophy is as I've described it.

Yes, yes, yes!!!! I know I've said I'd given up drinking. That was true but I changed my mind later and decided that I should just 'cut down'.

I suppose I rationalised the whole thing, but I really couldn't see what I was achieving by total abstinence. The exercise regime I'd self-imposed was tough enough without punishing myself further. Besides, I really didn't believe the occasional drink would do me any harm. Or indeed WAS doing me any harm.

I've never been a big drinker anyway...at least, not in my opinion.

Anyway, that was my decision.

Chapter Nineteen   Planning a Trap

How was I going to manage Collins's capture?

I'd do it like this:

An apartment would have to be bought, ideally in a large block and on the top floor, the penthouse. No problem. I had the money. Then I'd convert one room into a music room, which would have to be soundproofed.

Now the bait. I'd spend at least thirty thousand dollars on this, more if necessary. I'd recruit in New York. Bound to be someone. I'd offer the return fare, Business Class, to 'Oz' plus expenses and say a twenty thousand fee. I was sure I'd find somebody. Gays like Americans, I think.

To the casual reader, the idea of using an American rather than an Aussie homosexual might seem an extravagance, but just think about it. An Aussie might be 'known' to the local police and while Collins's henchman might not know the Aussie, they could easily find him. 'Money talks' as the saying goes and the Collins organisation would have plenty of that plus the desire for revenge.

A good-looking Yank would bring with him a *panache* that would appeal, I believed, to Collins. So long as I could get him here and then get him away quickly after his role had been completed, all would be well. An expensive exercise it was true, but well worth it.

I'd need to take my American to the apartment first, to establish his *bona fides*. I'd need him to have the 'feel' of the place. He could say it was his place or, better, he could say it was a friend's place and he had the keys to the apartment while the owner was in the States on a recording gig. Secondly, I'd need the Yank to pick up Collins and get him back to the apartment…no I needed to have got him into the apartment on the second meeting, the first meeting should be somewhere else. Collins would have somewhere for sure.

Then my 'bait' should be able to slip a 'date rape' drug into the wine, then give our captive an extra shot of something else to make sure. I wasn't familiar with the 'date rape' drug. I thought you could get it 'on prescription' for something else…and the 'extra shot' would be what? I wasn't sure about the drugs, but I made a mental note to find out.

Then I'd have to be called and together we'd need to move Collins into the soundproofed music room, and we'd tie him and tape him to a chair and to…something else, if necessary…so that he would be unable to move his head. Then the 'bait' would disappear back to wherever; New York if everything went according to plan. Then I would continue with my 'fantasy'. I suppose you'd have to call it that.

At the time, while I was making my plans, I often wondered why I wanted to do this. To write a novel and to get it published, say, or to get my gliding licence would be more enjoyable. Wouldn't it? And yet I think I'd made the correct choice. Without being in the military during a war, not many people have killed somebody, at least not 'in cold blood'. *Crime passionnel* was probably responsible for lots of deaths and then there would be deaths that were accidental - no, that wouldn't be murder - but quite a few deaths would surely be caused by overly aggressive actions or accidents in fights. I don't think many people would have committed murder as a highly planned exercise and fewer still would have preceded the killing with degradation, terror or torture.

I will.

I'm in a light plane. It's called a Piper Tomahawk and it's very small although it allows me to sit next to the pilot, who is actually a good friend from way back at school. The 'plane has dual controls and I have the…I don't know what you call it because it's not a wheel and it's not a stick but I'm currently the pilot. I suppose one should say 'I have control'! My friend is a pilot trainer, and he flies commercially but not the big stuff. Mid-afternoon, we take off from Manchester Airport, which comes as a bit of a surprise to me because we use the same runway as the one on which the 'shuttle' from London has just landed.

My mate takes off and we fly to a place called Sleep on the Welsh border.

After checking in and having a cup of tea (I would have preferred a wine or something) my mate asks if I'd like to taxi up to the starting point for take-off.

Of course, I say I would.

Then he suggests I 'take off'. I'm hesitant but agree after some instruction and reassurance.

Anyway, long story short, the next thing I'm piloting the bloody thing back to Manchester. My knuckles on the controls - like bicycle handles as I recall - are white but eventually I'm persuaded to take both hands off the 'Joystick' - I've just remembered the name, but I don't think pilots call it that nowadays - and feet off the pedals and the 'plane continues on its merry way without the slightest deviation.

Then my mate says, 'Well you got this far, - Manchester Airport's coming up, - so you might as well land".

Terror!

"Look," he says, "my hands and feet are inches away from the controls, so any problems…All you've got to do is aim for those lights," - it's dark by now - "and keep the plane at an angle so you can see both rows all the time. It'll set you up with the right angle to land".

I tense up but I do it! I land and brake and taxi to the hanger and am *unable to speak*. It's the most exciting thing I've ever done.

I'm up at a thousand feet again and my mate says, 'Well you got this far so you might as well land. Keep those two rows of lights so you can see both all the time".

I tense up but I do it! I land and brake and taxi to the hangar. I can't speak…

I'm up at a thousand feet again and my mate says,…

And on and on until the exhilaration subsides, and I choose to stop the scene.

I'm going into 'Phase Two' after this. Nobody's told me that because I haven't seen anybody, but I just know.

Chapter Twenty   Some Thoughts on 'The Wall'

I'd been going on with my training for nine months by now and I'd become amazingly fit. I was probably fitter then, in my late sixties, than I'd ever been in my life. It just went to show what you could do with a little bit of will power and application. I'd lost five kilos, which is exactly what I'd aimed for although I'd probably lost six or seven of fat and put on two or three of muscle.

What was going to be the 'stumbling block' for me was the so-called 'Wall'. They say you hit 'The Wall' and you have to run through it. Frankly, I'd thought that was probably bullshit - or, at least hyperbole - put about by experienced runners to discourage competition, but in fact, it was true. 'The Wall' existed and I was having a problem with it. I could run thirty 'kays' or sometimes a bit more, sometimes a bit less with absolutely no problem. If the marathon had been thirty 'kays' I'd have pissed it in. In fact, a half marathon would have been easy for me then…but a half marathon wasn't what I wanted to do. I wanted to do a *full* marathon and as a matter of fact, originally, I was thinking 'I just want to complete the course. I'm not interested in the position.' Now I *was* interested in position. I wanted more than just the ability to complete the course. I wanted, at least to be the first in my age group, or maybe the first in the age group lower than mine.

This was definitely a mistake, as you shall see. It was an ego thing, I know but the problem was that fucking 'Wall'. I needed to run through it. *Through* it. I kept telling myself it was only going to be once or maybe twice, sure, but I needed to train myself to have the will power, and the determination to do it and so I was going to have to do it in my training.

The problem was that the books I had read advised not to confront 'The Wall' until the first actual marathon. They advised limiting training to a maximum of around thirty kilometres.

I *thought* that 'The Wall' had occurred on many of my long runs; the pain, which was both physical and mental had kicked in and I'd just stopped and sat down and rested for up to twenty minutes. Then I'd continued, not without difficulty because my legs had stiffened up a bit during my rest, but that was something I couldn't do in the actual race. I'd have looked like a complete idiot. Maybe, I thought, I'd try a few more times and reduce my rest time bit by bit until I could manage without a rest.

Eventually, I realised that what I'd experienced wasn't 'The Wall' at all, it was simply exhaustion due to a lack of fitness. I came across a trainer at 'The Gym' who had run a few marathons and he confirmed that this was so. The only successful tactic was to face 'The Wall' when it came in a race, at about twenty miles and break through it. Did I have the will? I had my doubts, but I was going to try.

I'd booked my flight to New York. I thought that was the best place to recruit a 'bait'. I gathered there had been some changes since I was last there in nineteen eighty-two, but I remembered there were quite a lot of 'gay' bars in Greenwich Village. The guys liked to sing songs from the shows. I think that's a 'gay' thing. I was sure I'd find somebody to help but I'd have to put in a lot of effort because I'd only allowed myself four days in New York and although I'd stay a few extra days, if necessary, I didn't want it to *be* necessary because I didn't want to be away from training too long. We'd see.

The difficulty, as I saw it, wasn't going to be finding an individual willing to get involved in such a complex plan..., particularly with someone he'd never met before. Rather it was, first of all, finding such an individual with the physical and mental attributes I'd deemed necessary for such a project and secondly, someone who would be almost immediately available to travel to Sydney to instigate the plan.

I'd have to be careful and avoid jumping to quick conclusions. To select someone, later to reject them for whatever reason might leave me open to blackmail…or worse being immediately reported to the police as being someone recruiting for a 'hit'.

As I've said, I needed to be careful.

Chapter Twenty-one   'Saint Anthony'

When I think about it, which admittedly isn't often, I've never had many friends; acquaintances yes, but not many *friends*. I like to have one special friend at a time.

It was rather like my attitude to eating. Let's say I'd been confronted with a roast dinner - my favourite actually - and let's say the plate had held cabbage, peas, roast potatoes and slices of rare beef, there'd also have been some Yorkshire pudding, an essential with roast beef. There would have been gravy and, of course, hot English mustard and pepper and salt.

How would I have approached the consumption? Well, not in the manner that etiquette demanded!

I would have eaten the peas first then the cabbage - or possibly I might have reversed that order - then I'd have tackled the spuds, then the 'Yorkshire pud' and finally the meat and gravy and horseradish sauce. I'd definitely have gone for horseradish rather than mustard now that I think about it.

It's the same for friends. I didn't like to mix them up, so I'd usually go for single individuals rather than groups and the single buddy at the time we're speaking about was Tony Howarth or 'Saint Anthony', as I sometimes called him. You'll see why.

Tony was a Roman Catholic priest. I should say 'had been' rather than 'was' because at the time I met him he hadn't been acting as a priest for several years. He told me, however, that once you were a priest and had been ordained as such you always remained a priest until the Pope gave you the 'Papal Boot' - which apparently didn't happen too often.

I was in my final years with Comptex at the time I met Tony. He was working as an assistant to the Personnel Manager in a Company to which we were trying to sell a computing system.

We were having a few drinks in a pub. I seem to remember it was 'The Bridge' Hotel in Balmain, or perhaps it was Rozelle -

yes, it's Rozelle there - and Tony was sort of 'on the perimeter'. Somebody had made the point that The Catholic Church forced priests into paedophilia by its mediaeval policy of celibacy for its clergy.

Tony was suddenly there in the middle of the discussion. He seemed to have a 'presence'. I'll always remember what he said. He said, "You got it all arse-about-face! The Catholic Church doesn't make paedophiles. It attracts them. A normal bloke becomes a priest and if he feels horny, he gets off with one of the women in the congregation or goes to a brothel."

Cries of, "Well, you'd know, mate!" and similar observations along those lines ensued. Tony laughed at this then retired once more to the outside of the group. I remember being confused by their responses – I was unaware of Tony's clerical past - but I also remember being quite 'taken' by Tony and after subsequent meetings our friendship blossomed.

After some months, I made the decision - it wasn't a 'spur of the moment' thing - to tell Tony of my ambitions, my three things. I wasn't exactly definite about it; I sort of 'ran it past' him.

He saw straight through me! Probably his time as a practising priest had given him the experience to do that.

The interesting thing was that he didn't seem to have a problem with killing somebody who deserved it and of course, the marathon ambition was accepted without question. I suppose his Catholic faith ensured that suicide was to be condemned. We argued about that interminably. Actually, we didn't argue, we *discussed*. I enjoyed doing so immensely.

I'd told him my reason.

It was my favourite discussion out of many, the subject dearest to my heart, the final 'thing' in my trilogy of 'things'.

Strangely, Tony had no objection to the death penalty, in particular for those who had, as he put it, 'abrogated the sanctity of their own life' by seriously harming or killing one of their fellow human beings. He was particularly supportive of the death penalty where terror was involved, and he didn't mean 'terror*ism*'. What he meant, in particular, were those cases where torture or mutilation had occurred prior to the murder. These were, he considered most serious and particularly where the victim had full knowledge that their death was inevitable. I have to say that I agreed with him.

Where I didn't agree with him was on the subject of suicide. Tony argued for the 'sanctity' of life. I, on the other hand, believed that one's life was one's own property and just as one had the perfect right to destroy one's own wealth, so it was with one's life. I'd made the reasons for my decision quite clear to Tony but to no avail.

We argued - discussed - long and hard without either side convincing the other, which was to be expected. Still, it was fun, and it was amazing to me that someone could be so passionately against something that must have occurred millions of times throughout history.

After a time, I lost touch with Tony. He landed a Social Services job up in the Northern Territory and in his last letter he told me he had 'met someone'. In a postscript, he entreated me not to proceed with 'thing three'.

The next thing I heard was that the relationship with the 'someone' had collapsed. Tony had returned to Sydney, and we made arrangements to meet.

It soon became obvious that Tony, while being a really genuine chap, was overly concerned with other people's ways of life. Not a bad thing, I suppose if you are able to help in some way but a 'pain in the arse' if the impression given was one of interference. In my case, suicide, whilst of passing interest to me, became an obsession to Tony and the obsession was not with suicide *per se* but rather with *my* suicide. He just wouldn't let things go and I quickly came to the conclusion that if I didn't cut ties with him, he could have become a serious problem for me and for my plans.

I was not an unkind person, despite my wife having always called me 'insensitive', and it worried me to imagine how I could break with Tony without causing offence. The answer came quickly.

I was about to buy a penthouse apartment in the city, which action featured strongly and essentially in my second ambition. I would buy the apartment, secretly and quietly, move into it but leave my existing living place locked and unlit.

I would tell Tony that I was going on an extended holiday to Europe.

Chapter Twenty-two   Poor Judgment

'The best laid plans etc.'… How he discovered it I had no idea at the time, but a few days later Tony contacted me via my new mobile number, which I'd given only to the real estate agent and confronted me with, "I hear you've bought a city property." No mention was made of the 'European Holiday'! The source of his information, I found out later, was the real estate agent himself, unbelievably an old school chum of Tony's.

I made a mental note never to use that real estate agent again, a pointless threat since I would no longer be buying or selling property.

'St Anthony' was fast becoming a problem. My biggest mistake was to have confided in him regarding my ambitions. His Catholicism forbade his approval of my pending suicide, yet the possibility of my killing an 'evildoer' did not seem to worry him. It was as though his true belief system was akin to those of the priesthood who had used torture and death as tools of persuasion in the time of the Inquisition. Yet those same priests had believed that their methods would cause heretics to repent and return to the arms of the Church. In my second ambition, there would be no question of repentance or return to anywhere. My actions would be final. Tony's acquiescence to them was a mystery.

Still, Tony's beliefs were his own and none of my concern, except where they impinged on my intentions.

I had to get away from Tony. His concern for the 'sanctity' of *my* life was something with which I was unable to cope. I had somehow to alienate myself or remove him from my environment. The perfect answer, if I could do it undetected, would be to kill him, but to do so would be impossible. Well, it would be difficult, though I *could* do it.

My ambitions, particularly the final one, were paramount and Tony was in a position to spoil my chances of success. Yet I liked Tony, I really did. What was I to do?

I needed to do something, tell him something that would make him feel less warm towards me, less concerned with my welfare…but what?

Then it dawned on me; the perfect solution. He had told me that he was anti 'Gay marriage' and held the homosexual lobby in contempt. Therein lay the solution to what had become a problem. I would tell him that I was homosexual. If he became preoccupied with turning me back to 'normalcy' I would have the perfect excuse to become 'offended' and thus aggressive. I didn't want to upset him permanently. I would write a letter, to be delivered to him after my death explaining the reality and apologising for my churlishness. Yes, the solution had been revealed to me!

Now I began to worry anew. How was I to do it? And when? And where? To meet with him and blurt out, "I'm gay!" seemed inappropriate and probably unbelievable. I needed to prepare him. The timing would need to be right.

I phoned Tony.

"Hi, it's me. How you going?"

"Good," said Tony seemingly somewhat preoccupied, though I couldn't be sure.

"What're you doing?" I asked

"Er…watching the tennis. Shit!…broke serve. You good?"

"Yeah, I'll ring back, I…"

"No, sorry, mate, sorry, bit involved here," he laughed.

"You free Wednesday evening?"

"Sure."

"Fancy 'Hilda's?"

"Sure."

"My shout, see you there. Six thirty?"

"Great."

The conversation was over, the stage had been set.

Wednesday came around and I was seated with a drink at the restaurant table at six twenty-five. Tony arrived, punctually as usual, at six thirty and joined me at the table. He carried with him a bottle of non-vintage Moët et Chandon. Perfectly chilled, of course.

I greeted Tony, he sat down and after the customary pleasantries, we studied the menu.

"Having an entrée? Have an entrée."

"I will. The jamon Iberico, I think."

"Try the hiramasa kingfish carpaccio. It's beautiful."

"O.K., I will"

"And for a main?"

"Those split prawns, I think."

"Yeah, me too."

"Great minds…," said Tony.

And I came back with, "So they say!"

The waitress came and we placed our orders including a request for champagne flutes for Tony's bottle, which came quickly and bore a pleasingly icy frosting. A nice touch.

I'd thought that the appropriate timing would be to introduce the subject of my sexuality as we finished the main course and contemplated the desserts, but I was unable to broach the admission. Why I don't know.

We had both ordered 'sticky date pudding' and were considering a liqueur when I, almost involuntarily, said, "I have an admission to make. And you might not like my admission".

Tony murmured, "Intriguing," as the waitress returned with the deserts. We ordered the liqueurs.

The appearance of the waitress had thrown me a bit. What had, a moment ago seemed an upcoming statement with its own fluency, now felt as though it would be brusque and stilted. Still, I continued…

"Tony, I should tell you, I, er, I want to tell you, because I think it only fair…I'm gay!"

Tony's reaction was unexpected. He roared with laughter, loud enough to cause people at adjacent tables to turn their heads. I blushed.

Tony leaned forward and whispered, "So am I! We make a fine pair".

I couldn't believe it! Not that Tony was gay but that I hadn't recognised it. I suppose everybody is sure of their ability to judge others. 'He/She is a 'tightwad', a 'lefty', a 'perve', ambitious, lazy, self-centred, mean-spirited, lacking in hygiene, a gossip, a racist' and so on. On sexual preferences, we're all of us experts. 'He's a poofter!' 'He's gay as a paper hat!' 'Watch her, she's a bull dyke.' 'You know he dresses like a sheila 'atome'?' We've all heard it, we've all done it, said it. We all *know*!

Clearly, no we don't.

Apparently, *I* don't.

But what was my next move? Did he now fancy me? Had he already done so? Was I being conceited? Perhaps he 'wouldn't fancy me in a million years...daahling!' No! 'Gays', some 'gays', have loving, monogamous relationships but mostly they do what heterosexual men would like to do, which is have sex at every opportunity, and good luck to them. 'Gays' have it better than us 'straights'. Everybody knows that.

Tony leant across the table and placed his hand gently over mine. He looked darkly into my eyes, maybe not 'darkly' but he lowered his eyelids, before saying, "We can have some fun".

I fought to keep my hand steady beneath his, but I wanted to throw up. All I could think of was his sweaty armpits. Did he have 'sweaty armpits? All men do...I think.

I said, "Wait a while, I have to think. The timing needs to be..."

He said, "I understand. It's hard sometimes. I'll wait 'til you're ready."

"Thanks", I said.

I paid the bill, gave a tip and we left, going our separate ways.

Fuck!

Chapter Twenty-three   A Solution

Our dinner at 'Hilda's' had been disastrous. I'd completely, but *completely*, misread the situation. I'm not a bigot. I'm *definitely* not a bigot, so I had no problem with Tony's predilections and yet he had been so anti 'gay marriage' that I couldn't conceive of the possibility of his being homosexual himself.

A few days later I challenged him on this point.

Tony claimed that he was in no way alone in his feelings. Many in the 'gay community' were anti 'gay marriage', the feeling being that homosexuals, both male and female were quite O.K. as they were. Both groups enjoyed the fellowship of their own gender. They enjoyed sexual conjugation in the same way, whether with a specific partner in a long-term relationship or casually following chance meetings. Group activities were all right too. There was no need to hanker for the conventional by aping the 'straight' or heterosexual community. Marriage was between a man and a woman and that was that. Marriage was a quasi-religious construct, acceptable in its place but a construct totally at odds with the freer attractions of Tony's community. 'It was,' thought Tony, 'no coincidence that the term 'queer' had been generally replaced by the term 'gay' because that was exactly what such people were, gay, happy, fun-loving, out-of-the-ordinary, special…and *Fun!*'

His thoughts on the 'Gay Lobby' ran along similar lines. "We are here for but a short time," he said, quoting from some religious tract or other. "We don't need all that serious, self-regarding crap!"

I have to say I could see his point of view.

Nevertheless, I needed him to vacate my back and here's how I managed that.

Two days later I telephoned Tony.

"Mate, I need to talk to you."

There was a long pause before he said, with what could only be interpreted as innuendo, "You've thought…about it?"

"No!" I said, with a slight excess of enthusiasm.

"What then?"

"I need to talk to you about something else, something important."

"Ooh!" he squeaked.

"Yes, ooh! Come round tonight if you're free. No! I'll see you in the pub."

"Nine o'clock?"

"Bit late, but yes O.K., nine it is. Usual bar."

When I got to the pub, right on nine, Tony was already there, a half full schooner in front of him.

He jumped to his feet.

"Usual?" he asked as I sat down, nodding.

My heart thumped strongly as I anticipated what was to come.

Tony returned to the table with two beers. He sat down and swilled the remains of his original glass. He raised his most recent purchase and said, "Cheers!"

I responded and then said, "I'll get straight to the point."

Tony leaned back in his chair and spread his arms. His eyebrows were raised, and his face screamed quizzicality. Over-reacting maybe but exactly the response I'd hoped for.

"I work…for the Government", I announced quietly.

"Thought you worked in 'Sales' for a computer company."

"I did both," I explained and added, "now just the Government, not often now, just occasionally…I still have…contacts".

"And…?"

"And I need… I have to be on my own for a while, six months at least. I *have* to!" I looked furtively over my shoulder.

"Fuckin' Hell!" said Tony. He'd read 'between the lines' as I'd hoped he would.

"Yeah, after tonight…but we'll get back together after."

Tears appeared in Tony's eyes. He downed his drink, stood up and left, running a hand across my back, and squeezing my left shoulder.

What was all *that* about?

But it had worked. I very nearly laughed out loud.

I was to leave for New York the next day.

I'm confused.

I've gone into 'Phase Two' but nothing much seems to have changed.

I can still re-enact the most exhilarating episodes in my terrestrial life...over and over but I'm having some difficulty recalling any.

It's - I've discovered - impossible to repeat previous experiences. What I mean by that is if, for example, I wanted to experience my goal-scoring 'header' again it would not be possible.

So now, I've run out of 'highlights'.

I have arranged re-runs of two or three sales triumphs. Orders that were unexpected or so large that I felt sick with imagining what I'd do with the huge commission, but I've re-lived all those, over and over and I can't think of any more.

It seems now that the only things left are sexual experiences and frankly, I've tired of them, wonderful though I'm sure they were. But there seems to be a 'sameness' about them. I suppose that's what sexual activity is - 'sameness'.

Something - someone? - is telling me to think, to consider. But what should I think about? What is there to consider?

My life? The problems that confront the human condition?

I'll start with my life.

It seems to me that my existence was a complete waste of time. I had a good education, I was married, I procreated, I was a successful salesman in an industry in which the product sold itself. What else?

I murdered or was responsible for murder twice! Three times if I include myself.

Does that give me pause?

Not really, Collins deserved it and I chose the time, the place, and the manner of my own demise, but Annette...?

At the moment I consider her death, my action, was justified. She had a talent, she'd created things that, at the time - and still - I honestly believed she should share with the rest of humankind. I truly believe that my actions were the correct ones. Sad for her, sad for Anita but in the long run…?

But…yes, I'll have to think about that.

Chapter Twenty-four   In the Land of The Free

Well, here I was in New York where I'd been reminded of the arrogant, ignorant, unwelcoming, self-adoring attitude of the American Customs people. I remember it now from the nineteen-eighties when I used to go to the U.S., a lot and things didn't seem to have changed much. I suppose they were representative of their culture. What a pity. Such a great country spoilt by the people who live there. Insularity isn't in the hunt!

I wanted to say, 'Despite what you imagine, I wouldn't want to live in your lousy country if you paid me a million dollars,' but apart from trouble, what would that have achieved?

Sometimes I'm amazed by my own prejudices. The USA is populated by people of all shapes and sizes, all philosophies, and all political beliefs. Some are bastards, some are psychopaths, some are thieves, lots of 'bad people' but the vast majority are, as in the rest of the World, friendly and honest and 'good'. It's just such a pity that first impressions are so powerful and that it always seems to fall to me to be greeted in the USA by the 'bastards'!

It was late July and it was hot and humid as only New York can be and I'd walked down to Greenwich Village, which seemed to have changed a lot since I was last here. I like New York. I like it a lot. I think it's my favourite city…after Paris

I was sitting in a gay bar feeling somewhat 'miffed' that I hadn't been propositioned; not even approached, not that I wanted to be!

But there was nobody here that fitted the profile, so I left and moved to the next venue.

Now, this was more like it. It was really strange how the demographic changed from bar to bar. The previous one seemed to have been populated by 'wimps'. Everybody looked as though their day job was 'clerical assistant' or something like that. The bar I was in now seemed full of, dare I say it, more 'attractive' guys? They all looked fit, though not overly muscle-bound and they seemed to have taken more trouble with their appearance, their grooming and their clothing, all very stylish, without being outlandish. None of them was singing 'Songs from the Shows'.

Then I saw him. My bait. He was tall, very handsome, with bleached blond hair and a healthy bulge in his faded jeans. I watched him and the more I did, the more I was convinced that he was the guy I needed for 'the second thing'. He was surrounded by a coterie of 'acolytes'; all good looking but shorter than him. He looked like a Greek God. Blond curly hair like the statues, although I read somewhere that the statues were painted so the Gods probably had black hair like today's Greeks do; or maybe they used to be blond but successive waves of Arab attacks and migration had changed that.

How was I to make contact? Give him 'the eye'? Probably, but not exactly my skill, I'd look foolish and besides I expected I was relatively unattractive to gays. I didn't look rich either. I thought being rich would do the trick but although I'm sure that I had the money I needed for this project I'd never look rich, no matter what I was wearing or how well I'd groomed myself. It seemed like a note was my only option. It looked as though he was a regular in the bar. I'd leave but I'd stare hard at him while I was leaving. Give him a face to remember at least. I'd take my time. Come back tomorrow.

I did just that. I got up from my seat, walked toward the exit, slowed down and stared at 'Blondie' as I passed and received a response that was at first, querulous and then mildly aggressive. I responded with a slight smile, a Mona Lisa one, an 'all-knowing' one. I'd practised that in the mirror.

I left and walked back to the hotel.

The secret or so I'm told, of surviving night walking in New York is to dress 'down'. Jeans and tee shirt, scuffed shoes, no watch. I *was* dressed like that, but I saw no threats and suspect that if I'd worn expensive clothing and a Panerai watch the result would have been the same.

The next day I had intended to walk the other way, up to Central Park and go to the Metropolitan Museum, my favourite place in the city. Then I'd go to 'Blondie's' bar and put the proposition to him. He could only say 'No'.

And go I did and sure enough he and his group were there again.

My note read:

'Hi, I have a proposition, not sexual, I'm not gay but you might be interested. It involves travel to Australia and a <u>GOOD</u> fee for your services. Time in Australia would be two weeks max but your decision, then 'Goodbye'. Nothing illegal, maybe a little bit immoral.

Contact me on… (*I left my mobile number*) … if interested.'

I signed with just my Christian name.

'Blondie' was surrounded by his admirers as usual, but I pushed past them, ignoring the little squeals of offence, gave the note to my target, turned and left the bar.

Well, the line had been cast and the bait had been taken. 'Blondie-bulge-nuts' was on my line and the hook was set. By ten-fifteen the phone had rung. We arranged a 'meet' in a delicatessen on Forty-fifth Street at 3.0 p.m. the following day.

'Blondie', whose name, he claimed, was Tom Finn, although I suspect that was some sort of homage to 'Tom of Finland', a gay, comic super-hero icon, was a really nice guy. I was quite surprised because I was expecting an arrogant, self-adoring idiot. He was quickly responsive to my proposition which was simply to come to Australia, put up at a nice hotel, pick up Mr Collins, take him back to his hotel, have sex and make a date for a further 'fun' session two days or so later, which would take place at an apartment borrowed from a friend: me. I told Tom of Collins's background and his penchant for violence, which didn't faze him in the slightest. He thought that Collins deserved to be taken down a 'peg or two' and was confident that on a one-on-one basis he had the strength, the fitness and the martial arts skills to cope with any situation. However, he was equally confident in his own intellectual ability and believed that this, coupled with his sexual attraction would ensure that physical violence was highly unlikely.

Travel, Business Class Sydney, return to New York and accommodation would be covered as would be all incidentals. In addition, my proposition was that Tom, as well as all reasonable expenses, would be paid twenty thousand Australian Dollars as a 'consultancy' fee. I was strangely pleased when Tom argued for US dollars. I would have been worried had he not tried to 'up the ante' somewhere along the line. I agreed at a fixed exchange rate of 0.70, which was about right for the time. That would cost me just under eight thousand Aus. dollars more but that was peanuts if the job went well.

Tom was, indeed, a highly intelligent guy. He'd worked for some years on the academic staff at Harvard University. I assumed it was Harvard, but it could have been Yale or one of the other 'Ivy League' colleges; he seemed reluctant to be specific. His discipline (is that the word?) was European Economics. He had also been involved very strongly in the coaching of the University's American Football teams in the College League. I knew nothing of Economics, European or otherwise so I was quite unable to check out his story but his French was very good, and his German and Italian were superior to mine so I gave him the benefit of the doubt on the European Economics story.

Apart from seeing one game, some years ago between the Forty-Niners and the Dallas Cowboys at Candlestick Park I knew nothing of American Football either, so I took him at his word about that sport.

'Tom' - that wasn't his name, he told me that later but wouldn't tell me his real one - was, it turned out, a really interesting guy. He was on a kind of 'sabbatical', a break from his real world, which he tried to take advantage of every five years. He'd been doing that for the last twenty years so this was going to be his last one. He showed me a photo of himself as a university professor and I couldn't believe it. He was gay of course, he admitted that although there was no need, but his academic persona was quite different from the one he portrayed before me as we sat together the following day in a rather up-market bar on the Upper East Side. In the photo, he was dressed in a dark, well-cut suit and wore a subdued tie around his neck over a pale blue shirt. His hair was black with some grey in it but there was something about his eyes that didn't seem right. I remarked on this latter point, and he told me he was at present wearing coloured contact lenses. 'Tom' told me that his current status came as a result of his periodic desire to 'live on the edge'. He wrote romantic novels under a 'pen name' (a woman's) and was quite successful. He told me the 'pen name', which I recognised, but swore me to secrecy, an oath I intend to honour. When he went back to his real world, he simply dyed his hair back to black then cropped it short and spent some time in the sunshine to bronze his scalp. An academic returning from holiday, he would have already changed into more conservative clothes and life in academe would begin again.

We quickly came to an agreement and Tom was happy to arrive in Sydney in two months' time, the middle of October. He thought the project would be 'great fun'. I, of course, omitted to tell Tom of my ultimate plan for Mr Collins, which was his death. As far as Tom was aware, my aim was simply to humiliate the man and perhaps 'out' him as homosexual to society at large. I had told Tom that Collins had been responsible as a young man for destroying our family business due to my father refusing to pay protection money. My father had died early, and I intimated that Collins had been the cause of that tragedy. Not true but why spoil a good story etc., etc.

On my final full day in New York I paid a visit to the Metropolitan Museum and loved it as much as I knew I would. It was my fourth visit, and it never disappoints, you could reach out and touch masterpieces (not that you would) that previously you'd only thought existed as coloured plates in art books.

Afterwards, I spent some time in the company of the Alice in Wonderland bronzes nearby, then took an early, light dinner at the Russian Tea Room on West 57th, walked back to the Hotel and after packing, was in bed and asleep by nine o'clock.

I flew back to Sydney and into some very concentrated training. The Sydney Marathon was mid-September and I had around six weeks to prepare if I was to achieve my aim within the year, or just over.

My original plan was to run in the Sydney race next year or even the year after, but training had gone so well that I felt ready to give it a go this year. If I failed to finish, well, so what? I could back up next year by which time I'd be even fitter, and I'd have a marathon, albeit a failed one, behind me.

Chapter Twenty-five   My Training Continues

I trained as if there was no tomorrow. A walk to the gym; no hurry; a stroll, but it woke me up really nicely. I always had a cup of black tea and some homemade muesli - oats, almonds, walnuts, hazel nuts, pistachios, pepitas, lots of sultanas, milk, no sugar - before I left for the gym. Then machines and free weights, a kilometre swim, a quick sauna and into the ice-cold plunge-pool, back into the sauna, a shower followed by the walk home.

After lunch - always 'healthy' - a 'lie-down' for an hour, then a ten-kilometre run. Back for an early dinner ('healthy' again!) and an early night. Same thing every other weekday, then a complete break on Saturday. All I did was the shopping for the week. Then on Sunday, the big run; between twenty-five and thirty kilometres. No urgency, no straining, no timing, well, timing, yes, that was inevitable, but my target was to complete the course, not bust a gut. Then sometimes just a five-kilometre run on Monday or perhaps no run at all.

It's surprising what a few days' absence can do to a training programme. On my return from New York I coped reasonably well until the Sunday run. I was totally 'knackered' by the time I'd struggled to the end of it. I'd only been away a few days, but I reckoned it had put me back about six weeks. 'Oh well,' I thought, 'back to reality and back to the grind.' I knew I could do it and I knew that I would.

I say 'I knew I could do it' but at the time I started to doubt my sanity. I knew I wasn't mad, or at least, not completely so, but why on earth did I want to kill somebody? I wasn't a violent person. Perhaps that was the reason, to do something completely contrary to one's nature. But so what? What would that achieve? Well, it would achieve an exclusivity. Not many people, if you ignore the casualties of war, which you had to, had done that. To kill, not simply to attain a meal, is a human function. They say foxes kill for pleasure and it often appears so but it's not true. I met someone once who had a free-range chicken farm. In the spirit of research, this guy watched as a fox systematically killed several of his chickens, all past laying. The fox departed with his last kill, presumably to drop the 'groceries' off to the wife and kids but returned and one by one he dragged the remaining dead fowl through the hole he'd made under the perimeter wire. He dragged or carried them to a respectable distance from the compound and buried them, for future consumption. Clever.

No, not too many people have killed another human being. Mind you, I'd refuse to kill an 'innocent'. I'd kill someone whom I judged deserved it though and Stefano Collins was the perfect target.

Of course, the same things could have been said about running a marathon. The prospect was daunting, the reality would be, certainly, painful but it too was contrary to my nature.

As I've said earlier, I had not reached 'The Wall' yet and all my research, limited though it was, told me to avoid doing so until the actual race. This was why I'd limited my runs to thirty kilometres. It's the point at which 'The Wall' becomes a real possibility, the point at which the glycogen runs out and you start burning fat. But that's in a race. I'd been taking my long runs at an easy pace. After all, I had no desire to win or even get a good time. I just wanted to finish the course. Which is what every 'first timer' says.

Race Day was approaching fast.

Chapter Twenty-six   Hubris

It was very embarrassing although, surprisingly, I didn't feel that embarrassed at the time. I felt more embarrassed in retrospect.

The 'it' that was embarrassing was that I woke up on the Tuesday after the Sydney Marathon in a hospital bed. As my vision and therefore my comprehension cleared, I saw that I was lying with a collection of fine tubes and wires exiting my body and connecting with an array of instruments including a television screen. I lifted the bed covers and saw that I had been catheterised too.

Apparently, I had completed the course in a time just a little quicker than I'd hoped for, but I couldn't remember a thing about it. I have few friends and those I do have, acquaintances really, ('No man is an island!') had no knowledge of my competing, apart, that is, from Tony, who was under the impression that my first marathon was to be next year, and I hadn't said otherwise, so, thankfully, no visitors appeared.

I'm told by a nurse - it might not be entirely accurate - that after registering my completion of the course, I continued to run round and round the Opera House forecourt, occasionally entering the spectator crowd and then proceeded back up Macquarie Street at a slow jog, removing my clothes as I went. Finally, dressed only in underpants - no shoes or socks - I fell over and continued my journey crawling on very badly barked knees and hands…I can clearly see the evidence of that if I raise the sheets. The police 'arrested' me and called an ambulance, which quickly arrived and carted me off to the hospital where they put me in an induced coma and did their best to pump water into me in an effort to rehydrate.

Next of kin? No next of kin.

Well, what *can* I remember? The start? Yes, I can remember the start and going across the Bridge. I can remember that. And I can remember the first time I hit 'The Wall'. That was nothing.

I can remember running through that and I can remember realising that I was *competing*, and I didn't mean to do that, but I *was* and that had put my times out of kilter. I was running too hard, too hard for my capabilities. I wanted to finish the race; that was all. I had no need to get a good time, just finish.

I can remember Centennial Park and I can remember Pyrmont where I realised I was focussing on the back of somebody who was obviously a better runner than I, but I didn't want to admit it. I was trying to keep up with him and I shouldn't have been doing that. I remember that he looked like a runner; big, tall, skinny fellow, very sweaty. His singlet, I wore a tee shirt, was soaked with sweat and there was a dark stain down the middle of his shorts. He would need to drink at the drink stations. That would slow him up and perhaps give me the opportunity to pass him. I *shouldn't* pass him, and I didn't pass him, but I should have been running to complete not to 'place'.

Then I hit the second 'wall' and it was a big one. I'd never hit a wall in my practice runs, and I wasn't expecting two. I was timing my run badly.

I don't remember anything else. I guess it was at about the thirty-kilometre mark, but I can't be sure. That whole piece of my life has become a blank. I ran through the 'Wall' and didn't feel a thing. I must have done but I don't remember, although I must have kept going to the finish line. They say I did. The published results confirmed it. But I don't remember anything, and I knew my running days were over.

Still, I'd achieved a marathon run even though it wasn't London or Boston or New York. The doctors said I was lucky to be alive. They told me I should give running away. At my age, they said, I'd got nothing to prove. Well, I'd proved it anyway, but I felt so bloody terrible that I thought I'd take their considered opinion and 'called it a day'.

I'd reached the age when one needs to admit that the body is not designed to function forever. Is that a sexual thing? I don't think it is. I hadn't considered sexual activity for ages, at least not in terms of liaisons with others; in my imagination 'yes', but not in real life. And yet I believed that my other faculties were, potentially at least, in tip-top form. It's a mistake that many an older person makes and Hubris, as the Ancient Greeks had it, leads inevitably to Nemesis. I had to consider myself well and truly 'Nemesised'.

I was in the hospital for ten days before they'd let me go without protest. I still felt rough. But I'd done it, achieved a marathon, I mean.

On the eighth day in the hospital, Tony, 'St Anthony', appeared at my bedside. He'd seen my name in the newspaper showing the list of Marathon finishers. Why was he looking at that list? He'd been doing some detective work and had found me via the police and the medical fraternity. So much for 'confidentiality' but I guess that the disclosures were made with the best of intentions.

Tony brought me flowers and I was somewhat embarrassed by that. His present seemed predominantly to be zinnias or perhaps they were gerberas. They were in a basket. It seemed to me that flowers were something one brought to patients of the female gender or maybe if a woman brought flowers for a male patient it would be acceptable. Surprisingly, to me at least, it didn't seem to 'faze' the nurses who expressed their admiration. While Tony was there at my bedside - I was glad that he had come - I fell asleep. This I thought, on waking, had been rather impolite of me but I'm afraid I was unable to help it. Anyway, when I awoke, Tony was gone but he'd left a note saying he'd return the following day. I had, fortunately, convinced him that I had gone on Government business to Europe immediately after our last meeting. I said that I really needed the holiday after the 'other business' but had returned to Sydney just in time for the Marathon. My being away and my resultant dearth of exercise explained my current situation. He told me how proud he was that I had achieved my running ambitions and I told him that I too was proud of my efforts although I regretted my stupidity in entering, 'under the circumstances'.

After Tony had left and I had woken up, I spent some time looking at the zinnias, or were they gerberas? Their colours were stunning and that's not too strong a word. Were they real or had they been dyed? A nurse told me that they were gerberas, and they were their natural colours. Hypnotic.

I fell asleep once more, reliving what I remembered of my triumph. I read sometime later that no woman has ever regarded a bouquet of gerberas as a romantic gesture, so perhaps Tony's gift was acceptable.

Still, I felt more than a little bit embarrassed about how I'd finished up.

I supposed I'd have to put up with Tony for the foreseeable future, but I was sure I'd be able to cope. I'd just have to be a little more aloof and a little less accommodating.

I thought about the situation a lot and came to the conclusion that I needed to disappear, not totally but I should at least have alternative accommodation if necessary. I took a room in a boutique hotel in the city. More expense but necessary!

Chapter Twenty-seven   A Gun and a New Friend

Why I did the next thing, I really don't know. It was quite unnecessary and as it happened it was damned near my undoing.

I decided I'd need a gun, which decision comes under the general heading of, 'It seemed like a good idea at the time.' Subsequent events proved me wrong.

It's strange how the human brain works. I had absolutely no idea where I'd get such an item but once I'd begun research on the subject, I never considered the original premise again. I had to have a gun.

The permutations were enormous - automatic, semi-automatic, revolver, calibre, size, legal, illegal? All these things needed to be assessed and a decision reached.

But then, *obtaining* the chosen weapon. Should I join a gun club and buy one legitimately? Should I get involved with criminals and buy one that had been stolen?

What about the bullets? Where does one buy those? Do illegal guns come supplied with a number of 'rounds'?

These deliberations took me a lot of time and, I was intrigued to discover, a great deal of emotional effort. Why 'emotional'? I don't know.

Ultimately, I settled for a 9mm semi-automatic. The automatic, as I understand it, keeps firing whilst the trigger is held 'squeezed'. This seemed rather too dangerous for me. If the trigger was snagged somehow whilst carrying the weapon, say, in a pocket you might empty 10 'rounds' into your own body. Lethal, I'd say, whereas with a semi-automatic only one bullet is discharged if the trigger is pulled. One bullet in the thigh would be painful but ten would be terminal.

Now, what brand? Well, I settled on one, but I soon discovered that a customer who was in the market for illegal weapons, had little or no choice of make or model. One was offered 9mm semi-automatics of whatever 'mark' was 'in stock'.

The result was that a choice, of usually two pistols, was offered. Take it or leave it.

So, I approached it from the other end. I didn't want a Ruger, they looked cumbersome and rather ugly, but I was open to any other pistol that was on offer. In addition, I would ask for a hundred rounds of standard 9mm ammunition. Why a hundred? I reasoned that if I intended to organise an assassination, I'd only need four rounds at the most, so my request for one hundred might prove - hopefully - a 'red herring'.

I started out at a pub in North West Sydney. The clientele proved that I was in the right environment. I sat alone at a table studying the crowd. I can't say I would have trusted any of them. A small group of thin, long-haired, unshaven, and tastelessly tattooed men seemed likely targets. They each had the appearance and the air of being familiar with incarceration, some for lengthy periods.

I was planning an approach when someone joined me at my table, a rather powerful looking guy with cropped greying hair. He wore a badly tied tie with a white shirt beneath a dark blue suit and carried a fawn raincoat and a rolled-up newspaper.

He said, "Greetings from the filth!" and then, "Eric Baker, detective constable first class, and you are?" He offered his hand.

"Good to meet you," I said, "Mike Bevan!"

"Good to meet you, Mike. So you're not a poof, then."

"No, I…"

"Didn't pick you for one."

"No, I…"

"I'm off duty at the moment but I like to keep my hand in, as it were. Like to see if I can work people out. You're not a 'gayboy' but I suspect you're a 'pom'. Am I right?"

"Sort of. I was born there but I came to Australia in the sixties and…"

"Well, it still shows. Not much, but enough."

"Oh…"

"Drugs?"

"I beg your…"

"Ice, MDMA, cocaine?"

"No, not at all, I…"

"You see?" Baker paused to take a drink of his beer. He looked thoughtful.

"I see what?" I felt emboldened by his pause.

"I'm just saying, you're out of place here…you know?"

"Out of place, how?" I asked.

"Look around. Look a*round*!

I looked around then I said, "So?"

"Jesus!" my companion muttered. He leant forward as though seeking my confidence or being about to give me his placement assessment again.

I countered with, "You think so? I'm out of place?"

"I fucking *know* so! Look around this bar, they're all 'no-hopers', half of them, more than half have done time or at least are 'known to the police'. You're respectable. You've dressed down for this, but it doesn't disguise you. You're from the North Shore or the Eastern Suburbs. You have a nice home, wife, kids, and probably grandkids. Am I right?"

"O.K., nearly right…nice home, wife dead, kids, one dead, one pissed off, no grandkids…that I know of anyway. What gave me away? I'm interested."

"Your…demeanour, if that's the right word. How you look, how you stand how you sit, you know?"

"I…"

"You had a shower and a shave this morning, right?"

I wasn't too sure where this was heading but in a funny kind of way, I was enjoying being questioned and lectured and observed. I said, "Sure."

"Well most of these pricks didn't…and see how they stand? They slouch like it's too much trouble, standing up. They think they're tough. Most of 'em couldn't knock the skin off a rice pudden."

"Right," I said, "so I'm out of place. So what?"

"So what? So why are you here? I'd guess drugs but I don't see you as a user. You dealing?"

"You're joking. Anyway, what's your angle?"

"I don't have an angle, but I do have the ability to help, to give assistance, to facilitate."

"Doesn't exactly sound like the attitude of a…shall we say 'straight'

copper"

"Fancy another beer?"

The reality was that it wasn't the attitude of a 'straight copper', though just how much it wasn't, was to me, unrealised. I felt that maybe my meeting Baker was fortuitous. I had nothing to lose, and I had enough money coupled with a lack of possessiveness towards people or property to make a quick escape an easy proposition. It wasn't illegal to admit that one would like to buy a gun. *Possession* of an illegal firearm *was* and so, presumably, was buying an unregistered weapon, but expressing a desire to do either was surely not to be found as a subject in the Statute Books, whatever *they* were. Baker intrigued me and I wanted to 'sound him out'.

"You drinking schooners? If not, you are now." He laughed and sat down.

"Now…" he began.

But I interrupted with, "I need a nine-millimetre semi-automatic".

To say Baker was surprised at my admission would be an understatement but he covered his surprise well and assured me that this was just the sort of thing he could help me with. However, before he did so he wanted to know why I needed such a thing. I countered by asking if his assistance would be a 'one-off' because I would find a 'friend on the inside' most useful, especially one who could take care not only of himself but also of me.

Baker asked me again what I needed the pistol for, and I told him that he should get the pistol first and if that exercise was successful and if he wanted to proceed further we could discuss the matter. Baker was plainly annoyed at my response but didn't say so. He downed his beer and stood up, saying quietly, "Tomorrow night, here, bring six hundred. Should cover it."

"I'll need some ammunition."

"How much?"

"Ten'll do but if I have to take a box I'll take a box."

"Well, you ain't goin' target shootin'."

"No! And not a Ruger, I don't like Rugers."

Baker left and I left a short while later. My heart was beating fast.

Chapter Twenty-eight   Revelations and Anticipated Revenge

The following evening saw me sitting at the same table in the same hotel, a beer in front of me and a grand in my pocket. It was ten to eight.

Baker arrived right on eight, a sports bag hung from his left shoulder. He glanced at my table, took note of the level of beer in my glass and approached the bar. He ordered two schooners and brought them to the table.

"Your bag," he said, quietly.

"How much?" I asked.

"Five-fifty."

I felt in my jacket's inside pocket and withdrew a single envelope which I placed on the table saying, "Five hundred in there," and reaching into my jean's pocket, "and here's the fifty. What is it?"

Baker leant in towards me and said quietly, "Smith and Wesson M2 9mm."

"Excellent. Eight rounds?"

"You know your pistols."

I didn't but I'd happened to remember that from the internet.

"Rounds?"

"Eight in the gun plus a spare clip, fully loaded."

"Sixteen then.

"Yeah."

We toasted each other,

"Cheers!"

"Cheers!" and I took a drink of beer.

"Now," said Baker, "have I established what you might call, my *bona fides*?"

"I guess you have." I said, smiling.

"O.K.," said Baker with a hand 'chop' which plainly indicated the finality of what had thus far passed between us.

"O.K.," he said again, "where to from here?" The question was clearly rhetorical.

I waited in silence.

"It's drugs, right?"

"Yes," I said.

"I can help, I can facilitate. For a fee, of course."

"Of course."

"Go on."

"What if you're setting me up? What if you're selling me a pistol as a 'come-on'?"

"Good point. Fair point. I'm not but you're wise to check."

"How can I check?"

"You can't."

"Are you really a cop?"

"Yes."

"Is your name really Eric Baker?"

"No, but that shouldn't concern you."

"It does concern me. What is it?"

My drinking buddy looked exasperated though whether or not he really *was* exasperated was an entirely different matter. He reached into an inside pocket of his jacket and produced a wallet, which he opened and passed to me. I was greeted by my new friend's photo on a driver's licence bearing the name 'Clarence John Baskerfield'.

"And proof of your employment by the New South Wales Police?"

"Open the wallet."

"It's open."

"Right at the back."

I groped into the pocket he indicated and removed a NSW Police Identity card, bearing Baskerfield's photograph above the name Clarence John Baskerfield with the rank indicated as Detective Constable First Class.

"Baskerfield," I said.

"Correct," he said, "and your real name is?"

"Brooks," I said.

He repeated my name and then continued with, "Promise me one thing."

I hesitated, not wanting conditions, "What?"

"I work out of Camden, but never try to contact me there. I'm being investigated for something quite minor and I've got a lot of enemies. Poofters! Don't try to contact me there…O.K.?" There was a strong hint of a threat in the way he said this.

"O.K.", I said, "that all seems…O.K., but let me think about it. Can you meet me here same time in three days' time? Friday night?"

"Sure."

"I think we can work together. See you Friday."

I stood up and left Clarence John Baskerfield, 'Detective Constable First Class' at the table.

I thought that this relationship could be engineered to my distinct advantage.

The first thing I'd do would be to check up on Baskerfield's 'police involvement' and this I did. I'm not bad at accents and for the purposes of the exercise I would assume a Canadian persona. Now, an American accent is pretty easy providing you don't aim at a specific State or regional one. Most people outside the U.S. will accept a North Eastern States accent as generic American. I suppose it has something to do with American films. Most people too will accept the accent as being Canadian if the speaker says it's so. However, to really sound genuine, the generic American has to be modified slightly. 'Out' becomes 'Oot' or perhaps 'Oat', that sort of thing and any non-Yank who thinks they know accents will accept you're Canadian if you use these slight tweaks to the pronunciation.

I rang Camden police station.

"Hi there, officer, I wonder if you can help me"

"I'll try my best, Sir."

"Ya see, I'm oat from Canada and I want to contact a Constable Baskerfield or a Constable Baker. They were in

Toronto oat from Australia coupla years back and we kinda share a hobby, which is collecting Police and Army badges. They told me they were both stationed here at Camden. They still here?"

Not surprisingly, although I feigned surprise, the officer I was talking to was a Sergeant who'd been at Camden for the last ten years and had never heard of either of my fellow 'hobbyists'. He suggested I call the stations at Campbelltown and at Liverpool, which I said I would. To back up my story I did ring the Campbelltown and Liverpool stations with similar results although the officer at Liverpool did suggest another course of inquiry I might take, which naturally I didn't.

My 'helper', my 'facilitator' was not what he claimed to be. No matter.

Clarence (Clarrie?), (or was it Eric?) was a liar and clearly also a cheat who was out to take advantage of me. He believed I was involved in drug importation and saw my 'operation' as being 'ripe for the plucking'…by him! Why he thought that I had no idea. Maybe I'd unconsciously done something, behaved in a certain way, or said something that fitted the profile of such criminals. That was possible.

Whatever the reason, Clarrie - he preferred to be greeted as such - suspected that I was involved in the drug trade and that it was his destiny to profit from that suspicion if it proved to be true.

'Very well,' I thought, 'I will not disabuse him of his suspicions, I'll confirm them…and I'll have some fun'.

I knew that my life would be, like everybody else's, finite but I had the advantage of knowing - approximately at least – the date of finality.

Of course, I haven't explained this certainty yet. I suppose I should.

Perhaps I'll do so in the next chapter.

Chapter Twenty-nine   Some Doubts Creep In

I realise that this is the 'next' chapter, and I haven't forgotten what I said in the final line of the previous one, but I had a problem…quite a serious one, really.

'Tom' or whatever his real name was - I suppose I could have got to know it if I could have got a look at his passport - was on his way.

And I was getting 'cold feet'.

One of the tenets I had always lived by came from Shakespeare out of the mouth of Polonius in his speech to his son. It's a wonderful catalogue of advice, which culminates with the line:

> *'This above all, to thine own self be true*
> *And it shall follow as the night the day*
> *Thou can'st not then be false to any man.'*

Was I being 'true' to myself?

I was not!

I was contemplating the killing of a fellow human being, albeit a bastard, purely and simply for my own gratification. I was not 'judge and jury' nor did I hold any official legal status granted by the State. Besides, I had previously been opposed to Capital Punishment. As proof of this, I had been present, in spirit at least, in 1964 in the protest outside Manchester's 'Strangeways' prison when Gwynne Evans had been hanged and later in person outside Pentridge jail, Melbourne in 1967 when Ronald Ryan was hanged.

I used to think that all capital punishment, the idea that the State had the right to terminate a life in the most barbaric way was wrong. Nowadays I would tend to make exceptions for certain crimes, specifically those involving torture as a preamble to murder. As one ages one becomes less compassionate.

I was once asked to kill a chicken. The poor creature had been run over and was badly mutilated, its right thigh and foot mashed by a truck's wheel. I just couldn't do it and pleaded lack of experience in fowl despatch. Clearly, nobody believed me, I was suspected of weakness and the task was passed to one of the girls in our group, who completed it quickly and efficiently. I congratulated the executioner and said that I would have taken three or four times as long, resulting in unnecessary trauma for the bird. As I've said, nobody believed me and for the next day or two I was greeted with a variety of chicken noises.

And yet...and yet? And yet I'd killed Annette, with no qualms at all. How could I justify that? How could I rationalise that - as rationalise it I had - with what I saw as my firm beliefs?

The truth was, I believed, that the taking of Annette's life was justified and besides, there was no 'unpleasantness', no blood, no gore, no pieces of bone or brain, no smells. It was clean and it was justified.

I liked Annette; *more* than liked her and I hated my current target.

Collins had killed, many times, or had ordered the killing. He had tortured, he had, I felt sure, abused women but most of all he had insulted me.

This realisation 'pulled me up short'.

It clarified everything. I wanted Collins as my target because he had insulted me, or better put, he had hurt my pride. Was this a reason to kill somebody, that they had hurt one's pride? Would Castro Mulligan have reacted in that way? I think not but I was still unsure.

Apart from a slight, Collins had not done me harm. I doubted that it was in my nature to kill him or even torture him. Would it be in my character to avenge an insult by torture and death of the instigator? Besides, the insult, if indeed I had interpreted it correctly, had not been for my ears. I had merely overheard it.

Was revenge a justification for my proposed actions? Revenge for my perceived hurt feelings?

Or were my doubts caused by fear? Fear that things could go wrong. Perhaps Collins would overpower us. He was certainly strong enough and knew all the 'tricks of the gangsters' trade.

Was it simply cowardice?

All these thoughts, these doubts, were racing through my mind as I drove to the airport to pick up Tom. I'd had little sleep over the last few nights, and I felt somewhat 'shaky'. Perhaps I shouldn't have been driving.

I parked the car in the terminal car park and my mind was taken from my current indecision by the anticipation of an excessive parking fee, which would soon be mine. I smiled as I thought of the relative unimportance of parking costs to my present and upcoming situation. Old habits die hard!

I entered the International Terminal and checked the flight board for details of the San Francisco flight. Tom had told me that he would spend a few days in that City, doubtless so that he could check out the 'gay scene.'

The information directed me to the correct 'gate', and I waited.

Tom appeared quite early, which told me he had travelled at least in 'Business Class' and why should he not have done so? I certainly would have.

At Tom's appearance, all my doubts disappeared!

Some people have no presence. I'm such a soul. Others are noticed. Still others - and they are rare - have an aura. Tom had an aura. All eyes were on him as he walked down the exit ramp. People, mainly female, nudged their friends or relatives and indicated him with their eyes. Tom was handsome - 'beautiful' would not have been too strong a word - he was like a God or a medieval conqueror striding with consummate confidence into a grateful country.

Tears welled in my eyes.

We would capture Collins. I would humiliate Collins. I would kill Collins.

Chapter Thirty   Item 3 Explained. Item 2 Described.

I suppose that having completed the second thing it would be time to explain the third.

Yes, the second thing *had* been completed. I guess I'm putting it off; telling the story, I mean. I'm not quite sure if I should have done it really. I do know that I was a bit ambivalent about it. Was I proud, satisfied, that sort of thing? Or was I ashamed? It was difficult to be sure, one way or the other, at the time.

Anyway, back to the third thing; the final act, the swansong.

Cancer.

That was the explanation.

I hadn't got it, but I was nearly one hundred per cent sure that I *would* get it. It was in my DNA: pancreatic cancer. Both my parents and grandparents on both sides of the family had died of it, which was apparently highly unusual, six members of the same family! I reckoned I was 'odds on' to get it sooner or later. I'd already lived longer than both my parents and all my grandparents so I figured that my diagnosis would arrive soon. I couldn't be sure, of course, but having lived to the age I was, I felt that I had lived long enough, and it was my desire to beat the onset of an illness that would most certainly come. I'd seen the effects of pancreatic cancer and I didn't want them. So I'd kill myself.

Well, how should I do that and when?

The latter question was fairly straightforward to answer. I'd achieved items one and two. My marathon run had been less than spectacular, but I'd done it. I'd completed a marathon, a minor one it was true, but it was the marathon put on by the major city in Australia. It was the Sydney Marathon and just as gruelling as those in New York, Boston, London and all the others, maybe harder because it was a particularly hot day. I'd completed the course and achieved a result far better than I'd anticipated, even though, for the life of me I couldn't remember much about it, and I'd made a bit of an idiot of myself at the finish.

So, 'tick'!

My life as a tormenter and executioner had been a bit of a failure too. At least, it had failed to go quite to plan. Not that I had a plan as such but I'd rather imagined things to have turned out somewhat differently. Actually, I felt a little bit proud of myself as far as item two was concerned. I had achieved the desired result even if the means had turned out to be somewhat different from that anticipated.

Had I tormented? Yes, of course, I had. I had humiliated Collins, drugged him after cleverly entrapping him, imprisoned him, tied him up in a soundproofed room, had him at my absolute mercy and threatened him with violence. I had humiliated him and that humiliation, for someone of Collins' standing in the 'Criminal World', was torment indeed...humiliation at the hands of a 'nobody', a man of no consequence? Can anyone tell me that that was not a powerful humiliation, indeed torture?

I had not meant, at least at the stage in which it had happened, to shoot him.

The pistol discharged by accident, but he was not to know that. My apologies were thankfully covered up by Collins's screams, nay roars, of pain or perhaps frustration...humiliation?

What happened was this....

'Blondie' (Tom Finn) had arranged, by what subterfuge I couldn't imagine, to meet Steve Collins at a pub in Oxford Street - a gay hangout by all accounts - and after a couple of drinks and, I guess, some romantic conversation, take him to the apartment which he would say he'd borrowed for the week from a music producer mate. The 'mate' was currently in the States for some kind of musical 'gig' and would be away for a couple of months. The idea of a first and second apartment had been abandoned as having no merit, no relevance. We would use the same apartment, the one on the top floor, in which I'd had installed at incredible and surprising expense, a soundproofed music room.

The music room would not be used for sexual activity, that would take place in the main 'lounge room' in front of a very realistic electric 'log fire' and, bearing in mind the fact that I intended to leave the apartment vacant as I departed on my final project, I amused myself when I entered the premises the following day, with a 'puritanical' search for incriminating stains. It wasn't really *that* amusing, and it was probably a foolish thing to do, going to the apartment so soon after the first Collins/Finn encounter. Collins could have been having it watched, but I couldn't resist checking everything out and making sure all was ready for the big event. As it happened, no harm was done.

I had no idea how the friendship between Tom and Steve Collins was engineered but it was. Homosexuals have their techniques I guess, although my suspicion was that Tom would be irresistible once contact had been made. It amazed me that Tom had simply asked for the name of our target and that was that. No photograph, no address, no names of frequented restaurants or clubs. Nothing. Just the name, that was all that he needed.

Tom told me later that he had arranged a meeting with Collins the following week, actually in ten days' time, so he took the opportunity to fly up to Cairns and then drive to Port Douglas. He wanted to see the Great Barrier Reef; he was keen on both scuba and snorkelling, and he loved golf too. He had a handicap of six, so the little North Queensland coastal town was an ideal place for a brief holiday. I play golf or did, but I never got down to single figures. In truth, I never got down below twenty...well, twenty-three.

Tom had come back to Sydney, 'bronzed' and refreshed. He met Collins at a bar in Paddington and then, on Tom's insistence - he'd heard about it in New York - visited the Sydney

Bath House just for 'a look around'. I'd been told that they had a room there called 'The Suckatorium' with holes in a dividing wall but I may have been misinformed. Then they took a taxi to the apartment.

As planned, the first visit had been purely to cement the relationship and this they had done, I heard later from Tom, with the aid of some rather violent sodomy, though who was the sodomiser and who the 'sodomisee', I didn't establish, nor wanted to.

All went well and according to plan. On arrival at the apartment, early evening three days later, the wine was poured into pewter wine 'glasses', at the bottom of one being about a quarter inch of some kind of sleeping draft. I say 'some kind of sleeping draft' because I honestly don't know what it was, chemically, but I knew it worked because I'd tried a very small quantity myself and slept better than I'd done in years. Tom had brought it with him from New York.

Tom passed the wine containing the sleeping draft to 'Big Steve' who obliged by drinking it down in two gulps and asked for a 're-fill'. In no more than three minutes he was fast asleep, and Tom had made the call to me. I arrived at the apartment and together, Tom and I carried the burly and near naked yet comatose Steve into the recording studio and tied him to a very high backed wooden armed dining chair which had been fixed to the floor. Steve's head had been taped to the chair's back and there was no way he could have moved even a small part of his body.

The hypodermic syringe containing additional soporific remained unused and unnecessary.

Tom took his twenty thousand US dollars and left for the airport and a flight to 'The States' early the next morning. That was the last I would ever see of him; a pity, because he was a great guy and incredibly interesting.

Everything had gone so well. I was elated; more cheerful than I can ever remember. I walked with Gods. This was *me*, and it was so unlike me. I felt myself to be invincible.

When Tom had gone - he'd been into the apartment before the first visit and left clothes and belongings mainly in the master bedroom, which he had subsequently removed and taken back to New York - I got to work. Well, not immediately because it took ten hours before Collins woke up. I'd obviously underestimated the strength of the drug. When he became fully conscious, it was around seven in the morning and the anger in his eyes and the tortured twisting of his criminal mouth was something to behold and I knew that I had put him in exactly the sort of situation that was going to enrage him. Well, 'let him be enraged' I thought because in a couple of hours' time he would be a broken man, pleading for his life, which I would refuse to grant him.

I started by greeting him with a friendly "Good morning!" to which his reply was an angry "Fuck off!".

"Not a good start," I said and slapped him softly across the face. Now I suspect that anyone reading this story will ask themselves, 'Why softly?' and my explanation would simply be this. If I could slap softly, then I could slap with considerable force. All I'd done was to prove that I could slap him.

I slapped him softly again.

My captive's anger was rising.

"If you think, you little tosser," said Collins, "that you're going to get away with this then you're sadly mistaken. My people know where I am, and they'll be coming through that door out there any tick of the clock."

"No, they don't", I replied

"They don't what?"

"Know where you are."

"I'm glad I'm not you. You know that?" said Collins

"Why so?" I asked.

"Because you're a dead man," said Collins

I produced my pistol and showed it to him. "I think not," I said, "nine millimetre," I continued, showing him the gun.

"Cunt," he replied.

"I think not," I said again.

"I know so," said Collins, "and here's why…"

"Please continue," I said, reassured that the bindings that held my captive were going to hold and hold firmly even against the tremendous force of Collins's struggles.

"Because Fucknuckle, you have absolutely no idea what you're up against. I run this town from the cover of a very, very low personal profile. I don't make waves but when I want something to happen, it happens."

"So?" I asked.

"So, you'll pay for this. That I guarantee."

"I think not", I said yet again.

"I'll make you a proposition, I'll…"

"You're in no position to make anybody a proposition", I said.

"Shut your stupid mouth and listen and listen good! O.K.?"

"O.K.", I said with cavalier nonchalance.

"If," said Collins, "You untie me, I won't harm you, I'll simply walk out of here and I'll give both you and your Yankee faggot friend twenty-four hours to make yourself scarce. That means you go into hiding, the both of you. After that, if you're caught by my people, you *will* be hurt but you will live.

If on the other hand you cause me pain or kill me…no, you don't have the 'ticker' for that…but if you did, then you'll both die. You got that?"

I raised my pistol and pressed the barrel to the right side of Collins's nose.

"I admire your aplomb," I said, "but you see I have a slight edge and you're in no position…" Did I have the safety catch off or on? I could see the safety catch but wasn't sure if its position was 'on' or 'off'. I'd have to check that.

One thing was becoming clear, *very* clear - I think my producing the pistol had precipitated the clarity - and that was that I would be unable to kill Mr Collins or anyone else for that matter. It just wasn't in my make-up. I really wouldn't have cared if someone else had done the killing, but it wasn't in my nature to do it myself. This was going to promote a lot of problems. Where was I going to get a stand-in killer? There wasn't the time even if I knew where to look and yet it was essential that Collins died. If he was left alive, he'd be able to make searching for me easier. And it wasn't just me, Tom had to be taken into account and whilst I had developed tremendous admiration for the guy, I perceived a weakness in him. I'm sure that if caught, he'd 'blab'. No! Stefano Collins had to die, and somebody had to do it. As long as I had a head start, I could achieve my third and final goal, which was to die spectacularly though unobserved, but my captive could *not* go free.

"I need a break", I said.

I'd intended to remove the pistol barrel from Collins's nose with the utmost casualness but so concerned was I regarding the safety catch that I inadvertently squeezed the trigger. The safety catch was not on, and the noise of the report was 'ear-splitting'. The profile of Mr Collins' nose had been changed by the subtraction of a half-moon of flesh and cartilage. The resultant half-moon gap was bleeding quite profusely.

I felt a wave of nausea and started to apologise but my words were drowned out by my captive's roar of pain.

"You're a fuckin' dead man!" he shouted, blood bubbling from his nostrils.

I stood up and left the music room with somewhat shaky steps.

I tried calmly to evaluate my situation despite my desire to vomit.

I had tormented Collins mentally by his simply being in the situation in which he found himself and I had tortured him physically by shooting a hole - or half a hole - through his nose.

As far as he was concerned, I had done that purposely…even if that was not strictly the case.

I quickly closed the door of the soundproofed music room and went to the bathroom. I locked the door although there was no need to do so. I sat down, not on the toilet seat but on the edge of the bath. What was I to do?

And then all my immediate problems were solved because Collins died.

I didn't see that happen, of course, but I have absolutely no trouble in judging myself to be the cause of his death.

When I'd left the music room and its soundproofing, I could see Collins through the double-glazed window. He was shouting, I could see that, but I could barely hear him. I went to the bathroom and sat down. I felt sick and I stayed there a minute or two. Then I thought, 'Why am I being such a wimp? I've had the courage and the intelligence to ensnare one of the biggest crooks, nay one of the fiercest 'crime figures' in Australia. My intentions were to humiliate him, physically and mentally, which I've done so all that's left is to kill him, as long as I have the time to get away and kill *myself*, which I have.'

I got up and splashed my face with cold water and left the bathroom.

I hadn't meant to fire the pistol, that much was certain, but the reality was that I *had* done so, and Collins believed my 'action' had been intentional.

I returned to the soundproofed room and saw that Collins had his eyes shut and appeared relaxed even though his body and arms, legs and head were restricted by rope and gaffer tape. His mouth was a bit open.

I sat in front of him. Blood had dripped from his nose, from the wound, and stained his naked chest, though the flow seemed to have stopped. Some blood had started to dry in his chest hairs. He didn't move.

I waited.

He didn't move.

He didn't seem to be breathing.

I didn't want that, but it seemed to be the case.

I waited a long time before I concluded that Mr Collins had had a heart attack or a stroke or something.

Then I shot him through both knees.

What a loud bang those pistols have!

Chapter Thirty-one   Panic and a Mistaken Identity

I had to think, and I spent a long time doing that.

I left the music room and the dead Stefano Collins, changed my shirt for one of Tom's (much too big!) - there were some blood spatters on the one I'd been wearing - and left the apartment at around eleven, locking the door after me. I walked to the Intercontinental Hotel and sat in an armchair in the lounge.

I ordered a drink although, for the life of me, I can't remember what it was I ordered.

I sat, calming myself. I was panicking and I had to 'get a grip'.

After a few minutes, my consciousness returned and I looked around the room.

There were some very pretty girls at a low table nearby and over against the wall a girl sat alone. I noticed her particularly because she was very like the actress that played the female lead, 'Hanna', in *Whipsnade*. She could have been her double, or at least, her sister. Amazing.

I ordered another drink.

I would need to return to the apartment soon to tidy up and pack a suitcase in order to disappear. I estimated that it would be at least a month before anyone entered the apartment, by which time Stefano Collins would be somewhat decomposed. I was sorry about that, but I suppose somebody will be paid to dispose of the body so it's an ill wind etc.

I inspected the hotel lounge room now in some detail. I was scared, perhaps paranoid, that the Collins henchmen would be after me, although there was no way they could possibly know that their boss had been held captive and was now dead. Nevertheless, I looked surreptitiously around the room and saw no one suspicious or threatening.

I relaxed.

Some people, a group, had come into the room and had selected some armchairs in which to sit.

Then there came a man, on his own. I couldn't believe it!

I had never seen him 'in the flesh' before but I knew that figure, that face, that hair, that beard, those glasses... It was Mando Oliver, for Christ's sake! Mando Oliver, the man I would most have liked to be, or at least his character in *Whipsnade*. And he walked straight up to the girl that I thought looked like Hanna.

I couldn't believe it and I thought of Humphrey Bogart and, "Of all the gin joints in all the world she walks into mine". Although, this time it was 'he'.

Mando was taller than I'd imagined. He was very tall, in fact, around two metres.

I was excited as Hell but forced myself to keep calm. I don't mind admitting that I was obsessed with the man. Mando Oliver, the man I'd most like to be...or his character 'Castro Mulligan'. He really did look like 'Castro'.

Hanna - it must be her, although she looked a bit different in real life - was animated, understandably pleased to see the man she'd been expecting. Mando didn't sit and she looked up at him from her position in the chair with transparent adoration. Who could blame her? I tried to remember her real name but failed to do so. I started going through the alphabet but was stopped short just as I arrived at 'H'.

She got up and gave Mando a quick peck on the cheek. He picked up her coat, which she'd laid across another chair and passed it to her.

They made to leave, and I panicked.

I jumped up out of my chair and moved towards the exit. I wasn't quite sure what my intentions were but whatever they were, it was going to be my last chance to make them manifest.

As they approached, I acted as if I'd just entered the lounge.

"Mando!" I shouted and raised my right hand in greeting.

"I'm sorry?" he said, more a question than a statement.

The face was thinner, more drawn, the beard shorter and neatly styled, no grey in the hair, the voice different, more 'refined', perhaps British.

It wasn't Mando Oliver.

I apologised and withdrew.

It was approaching one o'clock and five minutes after the couple had left, I left too. I decided to walk south along Macquarie Street then cut through the Botanic Gardens to the Art Gallery and back via that bay whose name I don't know, to the Opera house where I thought I might have a drink at the Opera Bar.

I'd been much embarrassed by my recent mistake, and I needed to walk off my shame. I thought that I might be being followed. There was a shortish guy with a black hat not far behind me as I approached the Botanic Gardens.

I entered the Gardens, and my phone rang. It was Tom.

"Hi!" he said.

"Bloody Hell, Tom, this is a surprise. That was quick. You're coming through so clearly. You in the States already? No!"

"No, I'm not there", said Tom.

"Oh! What went wrong? You get stuck somewhere? You still in Hawaii? But that's the 'States', isn't it?"

"No, I'm still in Sydney."

"*What?*"

The guy in the black hat came level with me but then passed me, quite close, apparently unconcerned with my presence. He was singing softly to himself as he disappeared into the distance.

This was dangerous. Tom was the sort of guy that would be easily recognised. If Collins's mob were looking for their boss, which they would be, then Tom would be the key to finding him.

I imparted my thoughts to Tom.

"Yeah, well, actually…."

"What happened? You miss the flight or what?"

"Well the truth is I met a chick at the airport", said Tom.

"A *chick*? A young *boy*?"

"No a chicky chick! A girl. Couldn't resist it! Went back to her apartment in Potts Point. Wow! Talk about enthusiasm! And beautiful and rich, I can't begin to tell you…"

"I thought you were gay."

"Well, yeah, sometimes. I'm what you might call 'Bi', I just enjoy sex."

"Yes, I guess that's not uncommon but…"

"I know, it's dangerous and that's what I'm ringing about. I changed flights, I'm flying out tomorrow…or actually the next day. All cool! But I'm ringing to tell you I've actually been contacted by a Collins gang member…I think."

I suddenly felt chilled. I started to shake, not much but I was definitely shaking.

"You *think*? You *think*? Go on", I said.

"Well, I'm not too sure what the motive was but I suspect there's a bit of gang warfare going on and a bit of a coup on the way. I think Steve Collins might have gone into hiding."

"Did you tell this guy anything?"

"No, only where we went. He was cool with that."

"You told him about the apartment?"

"Yes, I mentioned it. I had to."

"Jesus Christ!"

"I couldn't avoid it, you know, and I knew you'd left the apartment."

"*How* did you know?"

"I rang your phone at the apartment, there was no answer, so I assumed you'd come to some arrangement with Collins and you'd…well, he'd gone too."

"You *assumed*?"

"Then I tried your 'cell'. No answer there either. I left messages."

"It was turned off."

"Well, there you are…"

I had to think quickly and normally I'm not the best at doing that but the answer, a story, came to me out of the blue.

I said, "I realised I didn't have the heart to torture Collins. We talked and obviously he felt humiliated by his being tied up. I agreed to untie him and let him go. He agreed to go with no hard feelings. He said he admired my guts. I'm afraid I was flattered and felt reassured. I untied him and he got up and *hit* me. Just once. I ducked a bit and his fist caught me on the side of my face. I have a fractured eye socket and he called me a vulgar name."

"Jesus!"

"Yeah, Jesus! But not 'Jesus'. Where are you now?"

"At my hotel."

"The one you had before?' I asked.

"Yeah."

"Check out and disappear. Go to the airport. Check in at one of the hotels there. No, go to somewhere else, then go to an airport hotel tomorrow night. When's your flight?"

"In the morning sometime. Day after tomorrow. Around ten, I think. It's with…"

"Don't tell me. Don't tell anyone."

"O.K."

"Just go. Go quietly and don't try to contact me again. Just disappear. You don't know what you're dealing with. Bad things don't only happen in New York."

"O.K., sorry."

"Just before you go, what did this guy look like, the one who contacted you, was it face-to-face?"

"Yeah, he was a little guy, dark, maybe Italian background…or Greek…or could be Arab. Smartly dressed, suit, tie, looked like a lawyer. Talked with an Aussie accent so probably born here."

"Black hat?"

"Yeah! How did you…?"

"Goodbye, Tom."

"Goodbye…sorry."

Then a thought hit me.

"Hey!" I shouted, "You still there?"

"Yeah."

"Tom, you did a good job, and I don't want you to think I don't appreciate what you did…but…can you do something else for me? I'll pay you."

"What?"

"I need to get hold of something."

"'Something'? Drugs? No problem. You want them here in Sydney or you want…?"

"Not drugs."

"What?"

"Explosives", I said.

"Jesus! What're you aiming to do? *Explosives*?"

"Again, nothing illegal, not even immoral. I can only pick it up in Winnipeg, Canada. Nobody will die, or even get hurt. Except me, maybe."

"What're you aimin' to do?"

"Can you help?" I asked.

"Sure. Take a coupla weeks. How much?"

"Make that a week. A slab of C4. Twenty grand 'Aussie', O.K.?"

"Ten for me, ten for the contact. I'll set it up today. Here's a number. You call it in New York. He'll set up a meeting in Winnipeg, or it might have to be in Toronto."

Tom gave me a number.

"O.K., no problem either way but tell him Winnipeg's best. Toronto I can do but I really don't want to, so Winnipeg's what I'm paying for. Thanks, Tom. Good luck."

I continued on my walk, my heart thumping at every shadow.

It was only when I reached the road that passes in front of the Art Gallery that I sensed the presence of someone to my left and just behind me. I turned my head slowly. It was Baskerfield.

"Jesus!" I jumped.

"Close," he countered and laughed.

"How long've you been there?"

"Since you set out, a bit further back, but. Looking after you. Unpaid, unrewarded."

"I don't need 'looking after' as you so quaintly put it."

"Oh, yes you do! See that guy in the black hat that overtook you? Who d'you think that might have been?"

Intrigued, I said, "No idea."

"That, dear friend, was one of Collins's men. Fucked off when he saw I wasn't going to get lost myself. You done something to upset Collins? Hope not, for your sake. You haven't crossed him in a deal, have you?"

"No. A deal? I don't even know who Collins is so why would one of his mates be after me?" I asked.

"No idea, but he looked interested in you. Maybe I've saved your life already. We should come to an…arrangement."

'Yes', I thought, 'indeed we should…and indeed we will.'

"Look," I said, "I apologise, I appreciate what you did back there, you probably did save my life. Will you join me for a drink back at my hotel? We can talk some business."

He replied simply and succinctly, "I will. But let me ask you a question."

"O.K."

"Who were you on the 'phone to? Sounded a bit…" He spread his hands and waggled them; a gesture that in the context of our conversation, made his meaning clear.

I answered, as mysteriously as I could, "A colleague. An American who lives in New York".

Baskerfield said nothing and we walked on.

It was some days later, after arrival in Toronto that I read in the local press that three nights after my last conversation with Tom, around one a.m., well after the curfew had begun and when only the cleaners were in the baggage collection area of Sydney Kingsford Smith International Airport, one of the central carousels started up. Some words of surprise were exchanged in Korean but otherwise the incident was ignored. After about a minute a blond head appeared above the feeder chute followed by a partially clothed very athletic looking body. The body, its throat cut, tumbled onto the conveyor and was swept away on a never-ending journey around the carousel. The Korean cleaners looked on in astonishment. The report said that the blond-headed body was thought to be an American citizen.

I'm thinking.

I'm not re-living anything now. Sex 're-plays' have been a disaster. Quite boring after a while, though exciting when they happened, in my life 'on earth', if I remember correctly.

I'm starting to feel frustrated now and yet I'm still happy. Incongruous!

I've thought about my life…uninteresting…and yet…

What about love? I mean being 'in love'.

That happened to me a few times, though it was largely unrequited, or it was after a few weeks. People get bored with each other.

Still, I'll try to think about it.

I've thought a lot about Annette. My conclusion is that what I did, what I achieved, was necessary. So that's that! Anyway, so what? No retribution here.

Chapter Thirty-two   A 'Partnership' Confirmed

Back at the hotel with Baskerfield (call me 'Clarrie'), I suggested the bar, a quiet place, little used by the guests though very stylish in the way of 'days-gone-by'. Alternatively, I had offered my room on the fourth floor. We could have used the mini-bar and if required, a room service meal. Baskerfield had looked doubtful, I don't know why.

We settled on the bar, a warm, welcoming room, the mahogany chairs upholstered in a kind of dark red velvet, the polished timber of the low tables protected by polished glass. On the walls were excellent prints of 'Olde English' hunting scenes. The carpet was largely dark red and discretely floral.

A waiter came mincing towards us, gave us each a 'snack menu' and took our drink orders. When he returned with our drinks both of us ordered the steamed Chinese dumplings.

Once the waiter had gone, Baskerfield said, "Now!" and leant back in his chair, raising quizzical eyebrows.

"O.K.", I said. "You were right."

"Drugs?"

"Drugs."

"What sort?"

I'd thought about that. To say the wrong thing at this stage might show my ignorance.

"We're flexible", I said.

Baskerfield seemed to accept that, and I painted a picture of a very sophisticated organisation based in Jakarta of which, due to my connections (which in reality were non-existent) I had become the head honcho in Australia and New Zealand.

Baskerfield questioned that. He said I was the most unlikely person for that sort of job he'd ever seen. To which I responded by saying that the reason I'd been selected was precisely because of that. He didn't look convinced, and I realised I would need to show more *bona fides*.

"You mentioned Collins earlier," I said.

"So?"

"So, you seen him lately?" I asked.

"No, but so what?"

"You won't be seeing him again."

"Why's that?"

"He's dead."

"Bullshit."

"I got rid of him."

Baskerfield broke into roars of laughter. Knowing more about Collins than I had when I'd started this project, I could understand his amusement. However, I kept a straight and serious face.

"I can understand your incredulity, Clarrie," I said quietly, once Baskerfield had calmed down. "I'll give you some details which I hope will convince you," and I proceeded to do just that, avoiding the existence of what he would see as simply my 'bucket list'. I told him that there had initially been some misunderstanding between myself and Collins which had developed into antagonism and finally, out and out war, albeit the argument had always been kept between the two of us with no other parties involved. Eventually, it had become obvious that one of us would need to be eliminated and it wasn't going to be me.

"Did you know that Collins was a 'pillow biter'?" I asked using one of Baskerfield's own expressions.

"I'd heard rumours," my companion replied, although he was not convincing.

I told him the whole story, near exactly as it had happened, my visit to New York, the involvement of Tom, the capture, the drugging, and the *finale* of Collins's death. I freely admitted the heart attack that proved the death of my competitor but claimed the shooting through the nose had been intentional. The shooting through the knees had, I admitted, been carried out post-mortem and I said that this was done in order to send a message to Collins's troops. Clearly, at least one of the 'troops' had not been warned off by my action.

Here was my salvation. Well, that's a bit of an exaggeration but if I was careful, I could use my 'pretend cop' to my advantage. With Baskerfield's companionship, I would be less vulnerable from all comers but especially Mr Black Hat who would be hesitant to attack if I had a large thug - i.e. Baskerfield - by my side.

I had told Baskerfield that I trusted him implicitly but made him swear confidentiality with what I'd already told him as well as what I was about to disclose. We had our 'agreement'.

I guessed that he'd not seen the inside of a church for many years, if ever, but he insisted on giving his assurances, 'As God is my judge!' he further swore on the life of his mother. It was a risk, I know, but I thought, a risk worth taking, and my circumstances would make it relatively easy to extricate myself if it became necessary.

I said that the 'merchandise' was 'ice' and that it was planned to get it into the country via Sydney Heads and the Spit Bridge. The origin of our cargo was Jakarta, and we would need to pay 'up front'.

I told him too about the very complex money moving arrangements.

We would use the Islamic Hawala system, which is a very flexible money moving arrangement, usually but not exclusively, between Muslim countries. I described the system to Baskerfield in some detail and confirmed that it was ostensibly for the Islamic community but that there was considerable flexibility.

I said that I held an account with a U.K. bank from which I would access one million U.S. dollars, which would then be transferred to Jakarta via the Hawala system. This part of the operation would be mine although I intended to think up an excuse for not going and sending Baskerfield in my place. This latter information I did not, of course, pass to my new friend.

Transportation of the 'goods' was to be carried out using two boats, one from Indonesia and a smaller one from Sydney which would be leaving the Spit in Sydney Harbour around five p.m. 'for an evening sail to Pittwater'.

The 'Marine Rescue' organisation would be notified of all moves including a false one advising entry to Pittwater at the completion of the journey. In reality, a rendezvous with the Jakarta boat would be arranged several kilometres off-shore where the 'ice' would be transferred late at night. After that, we would sail to Pittwater and the following morning would return to 'The Spit' keeping 'Marine Rescue' informed of our every move.

I told Baskerfield that that was all I was prepared to disclose at this point except to say that I would be 'skippering' the Sydney one and that I was a very experienced sailor.

He 'understood completely' and said so. He was with me 'one hundred per cent' but he also suggested that I might prefer that he took charge of the pistol.

I had to admire his 'front'. I had bought the pistol plus the ammunition from my new 'bodyguard' who had doubtless made a substantial profit on the deal. He was now suggesting I return the weapon to his care with a view to his using it for my protection. I knew that I'd never see the pistol again. I doubt that the weapon would accompany him on the journey I had planned for him since it would involve air travel. Baskerfield was not stupid enough to risk that. But he would doubtless hide the weapon before leaving Australia. All things considered, the outcome would be to my benefit. I really didn't want to take responsibility for the pistol. My buying it had been a mistake.

The following day I gave him the pistol.

I met with Clarrie Baskerfield almost on a daily basis after that and I saw no more of Mr Black Hat although, in retrospect, I imagine he saw lots of me.

Two weeks after our initial 'agreement', Baskerfield was becoming tiresome, I had little in common with him, having no real interest in boxing, golf, pornography or drinking vast quantities of beer. I claimed that I needed a weekend to myself. The implication was that a woman was involved.

Baskerfield tapped the side of his nose and said he'd see me on Monday.

On Monday I telephoned and told him I was urgently needed in Jakarta. There was a technical problem that only I could solve. I apologised for not having kept him 'in the loop' by not disclosing my exact programme but I said I was due to fly to London the next day (Tuesday) to arrange for the money transfer. Under the new circumstances I was afraid that Clarrie - by now we were firmly on first-name terms - would need to go to London in my place and asked if he would be comfortable doing that? As expected, he jumped at the chance, particularly when I told him that he was to withdraw one million and twenty thousand US dollars or its equivalent, of which one million was to be transferred to Indonesia with the balance for him to buy a business class ticket back to Sydney plus any other expenses he might encounter. With such an offer it was no surprise that he readily agreed.

I gave him all the account numbers and passwords I told him that he would need, including how to organise a Hawala deal and told him that a business class ticket on an Emirates flight to Manchester would be given to him as I took him to the airport on Tuesday morning. Manchester had been selected for security reasons and he would need to make his own way down to London to visit the bank and get the money.

Someone with the I.Q. of a fence post would have seen the holes in my instructions and would have seen the stupidity of the procedures but Baskerfield didn't. I guessed that he wouldn't because he was driven by his lust for importance and the programme I'd set for him gave him both that and money to flash around. Had he questioned me, however I had fulsome praise ready for him. I would have told him how impressed I was with his perspicacity and then told him the 'real' plans, which naturally would still ensure his flying to England.

The bank existed, though of course the account did not. Tony would be stranded in London with little money for a while. He would need to pay his own fare back and his understandable intent would be to locate me and wreak revenge. I would be nearly untraceable and, in any case, likely deceased.

After leaving him at the airport, I told him I would drive back to my apartment, pack and return to the airport the next day in order to catch the early flight to Jakarta.

When Clarrie had checked in his baggage and left to go through Customs, I'd never seen him so happy. His mood would change after the first contact with the bank but by then I'd be on my way to Canada.

I believed I would never see Clarrie Baskerfield again though as it turned out, he nearly proved my undoing. He'd nevertheless, served me well. He'd kept Mr Black Hat away and for the most part, had been rather pleasant if intellectually limited company.

The whole exercise had been an interesting challenge, but it worried me that I'd enjoyed being rather cruel to someone who at face value was solely concerned with my welfare. His fault though…he shouldn't have told me he was a policeman.

Chapter Thirty-three   Travel Plans and Paranoia

Back at the hotel - I seemed now, to be spending most of my time there - I collapsed onto the bed and assessed my situation. Everything had gone, pretty much, to plan. I had my flights to Canada organised, the apartment had been cleared out and the front door securely locked. Tom had told one of Collins's men the whereabouts of the apartment but as far as I could see there was no need to worry. Anyone wishing to gain entry would need to force the door, which I didn't imagine they would do, not in the first instance anyway. Eventually, of course, entry would be made, and the body of Steve Collins would be discovered but by then I would be long gone, possibly already dead by my own hand.

I realised, of course, that I had been foolish to target Collins for my second 'thing'. Here was a man with the backing of a very strong - well, 'military force' would not have been an unreasonable description - plus possibly hundreds of rather unsavoury people keen to assist and I had been stupid enough to think I could kill the man with no repercussions. It would have been far simpler, and much safer to have targeted, say, a serial killer or a paedophile, if either could have been located. Even then, it would certainly have been problematical, probably impossible; a serial killer would either be unknown or in jail and a paedophile would have been too easy. I don't like paedophiles although I've never knowingly met one. They're mostly sad people, I'd guess, not real bastards.

Whatever course of action, whatever criminal 'profile' would have been the more suitable, I certainly hadn't thought the problem through. I realised Collins had been selected solely on the basis of his having humiliated me in the hotel bar. My targeting Collins had been no more than revenge for that, and I was now paying the price of the decision. They that live by the sword etc….

With Baskerfield *en route* to London I thought I'd better check my tickets again. I couldn't afford errors.

I got up from the bed and opened my suitcase. I inspected the pocket.

Nothing.

As I rushed to the chest of drawers, I felt my heart beating and my chest contracting. I looked in all the drawers.

Nothing.

My passport and tickets were gone.

Holy Hell, what an idiot! Passport and tickets were in the apartment, in a drawer of the kitchen's 'breakfast-island'. I'd left them there over a week ago between Tom's first and second visit and forgotten all about them. I'd come straight from the travel agents in King Street and was checking out the apartment. I'd put all the documents out of sight…just in case. There was so much on my mind, and I was so stressed that I thought I'd brought them back to the hotel and put everything in the case. Then I thought, 'Hey, wait for a sec., I've got a room safe, I'd have put everything in there!'

I went to the cupboard that housed the safe and entered the code that I foolishly use for everything. It's a date that by deducting the zeros and/or the '19' of the year date I can make it eight digits or six or four. The door buzzed and opened. Inside there were one thousand six hundred dollars, which I'd completely forgotten about, and my spare car keys but nothing else. I'd have to return to the apartment.

And return I did.

There were some workmen doing something to the front door of the building - I think it hadn't been swinging quite properly - but apart from them I saw nobody. I entered the lift and used my card to give me access to the buttons. I went to the top floor, the penthouse level and inspected my door. There was no evidence of forced entry. I unlocked the door and went in. All was quiet.

I glanced toward the music room. Collins was still there but looking paler and somehow sadder.

I moved to the kitchen and registered the black straw-weave trilby hat sitting on the dining table. When had I left that there or rather, where had it come from? I didn't think I had such an item although I do have a lot of hats. I think hats suit me. I've got a lot of 'baseball hats' for example. They're from my years of membership of the Sydney Swans. I have floppy brimmed hats, they're better to keep the sun off and I think I still have a couple of trilbies and a couple of 'flat caps' but I don't remember a hat like the one on the table. Maybe Tom had had such a hat. Maybe he'd left it.

In the kitchen I moved to the breakfast island and opened the drawer in which I'd expected to find all my travel documents. As expected, and to my great relief, they were all there but somewhat disarranged.

Now, I'm a bit obsessive about neatness and the reason is this: when I was seventeen I got my first job. Jobs were easy to get at the time. There were plenty of jobs but plenty of applicants too and labour conditions weren't like they are today. Firing without redress was as easy as hiring, there were no Government departments to which one could appeal an unjustified dismissal. I was fired for simply having a cluttered desk. I suspect there were other things, perhaps in my general attitude where I was lacking but that was the reason given. It upset me at the time because I knew exactly where everything was on my desk, cluttered or not, and I believed that justice had not been served. I did, however, come to accept the incident as a lesson learnt and since that time I'd valued neatness as a positive characteristic. Everything, paperwork especially, was put into piles with individual items related to each other. Sequence was important too, so, for example, my passport, being the first item needed at check-in would be at the top of the pile and so on. As far as sequence was concerned, everything was as it should be but there was something that told me that my travel pile had been disturbed and not by me!

One of my obsessions was that everything should be aligned left and that the top left-hand corner of each item should be aligned too. This was very definitely not now the case, and I could only conclude that my documents had been disturbed.

And then I remembered the hat. I certainly didn't possess such a thing. I owned lots of hats but none that were shiny and black and coarsely woven. It's a sad fact of life that as one ages, one's thought processes become slower. It has nothing to do with Alzheimer's or senility, although one could argue for the latter, it's just part of aging, like getting the body started immediately on rising. After about fifty there's a gradual decline both physically and mentally. It probably starts earlier than fifty. They say ('they' do) that after forty a man loses one per cent of the body's testosterone each year. Not many would agree but I consider that a 'positive'!

The hat? Why hadn't my 'visitor', if indeed there had been one, taken it with him? Had he forgotten it? Was it left as a message?

Or maybe he was still in the apartment!

I panicked, grabbed the travel documents and without attempting to verify the foreign presence, or otherwise, hurriedly left the building.

I jogged back towards my hotel, then, changing my mind, crossed the road and walked back to a café opposite the apartments, entered, ordered a coffee, and sat at a table, not in the window but one which gave me a clear view of the building and waited.

I didn't have long to wait. Through the front doors of my apartment block there emerged the black shiny hat atop the head of a small, swarthy complexioned man of around fifty. Maybe he'd been in the bedroom or the spare one, maybe under a bed, maybe in a wardrobe, who knew? It was academic anyway. Whoever it was - and I suspected it was the same man who had contacted Tom - he now knew that Collins was dead and that I was about to make my escape to Canada on a particular airline and at a specific time.

Of course, I would have to change my itinerary, cancel the direct-to-Canada trip, and make new reservations. I went back to the Travel Agent and not without some embarrassment, cancelled and re-booked. I was actually surprised that the travel agent expressed no agitation in response to my requests. He was, in fact, totally obliging and I came away with a new itinerary starting on the same day but later: Sydney, Melbourne, Sydney, Dallas. I told the travel agent that I needed to finalise some business in Melbourne before flying out. I'd hire a car in Dallas and drive to Houston. I intended to book a flight north from Houston after I'd booked into the hotel reserved for me by the travel agent and from wherever the flight was booked to, probably New York, proceed by train or coach to Toronto then hire a car for the completion of my journey to Manitoba. The reason I'd asked for Melbourne to be included in the ticketing was that I would depart from the Domestic Terminal rather than the International, which would, of course, be watched.

I realise my actions displayed marked paranoia, but I'd always been the careful type and I was keen to avoid contact with Collins's goons.

What has come as a complete surprise to me is that Hell is a pure fiction of the established churches. The truth is, Hell, or indeed Purgatory, does not exist. I had anticipated punishment, albeit probably minor, for the occasional transgressions during my middle age, both social and commercial but I was particularly concerned with what I'd done to Annette. Surely, I would be made to pay. But no! Nothing!

Had I known this I would probably have transgressed more. As I've told you, the place I'm in allows no social contact. One doesn't need that. But I know that I'm here with the thieves, the rapists, the murderers, the vain and the self-obsessed as well as the honest, the upright, the charitable and the good. Nobody here is judged.

It's interesting to me now that in 'life' I had contemplated Heaven and Hell on many occasions and compared them to various situations to which humans are subject.

What interests me now is that I know - how do I know? - that I'll receive a gift at a time called 'The Gifting' towards the end of my stay in 'Phase Two' and naturally I'm intrigued. What will it be? What do I want?

In my terrestrial life, I wanted many things...a bigger house, a better view, a Mustang car, an AC Cobra - an original model - a Ducati motorbike or an original Triumph Bonneville, a Gibson guitar, the list was endless but in my current situation could I use such things?

Perhaps now, the 'gift' would be intellectual in nature and yet I felt that with the ultimate in happiness on the horizon, what else could I want?

Chapter Thirty-four   Off I Go (My Destiny Awaits)

The flight to Melbourne was uneventful, except that I thought I saw Mr Black Hat at Sydney Domestic Terminal but I'm sure I was mistaken. The guy in question wasn't even wearing a hat, he just walked past the waiting gate area for my flight. He didn't even look at me and certainly I had seen no evidence of being in any way 'under surveillance'. He looked like the guy though.

I took a taxi into Melbourne, bought a cup of coffee then returned to Tullamarine for the flight back to Sydney. On arrival, I transferred to the International Terminal and went immediately to the Business Class lounge where I had to endure a three-hour wait for the Dallas flight. I had contemplated travelling First Class. I could have afforded it but considered it an extravagance.

I read *The Australian* and flicked through a magazine called *Men's Health* then returned to the newspaper-and-magazine rack and picked up the *Daily Telegraph*, not a paper I'd normally read - a bit 'sensationalist' - but there was an article in that paper concerning the *Gangs of Sydney* and to my surprise, there was Stefano Collins's picture - no mention of his demise - together with several pictures of Collins's off-siders; and there amongst the 'gallery' was Mr Black Hat whose *nom de guerre* was Kevin ('Kev') 'Handyman' Thompson, the nickname a reference to his willingness to take on 'special' assignments.

We boarded on time but then were forced to wait an hour on the tarmac, whilst an emergency was dealt with. The 'emergency' apparently did not come to fruition and off we flew.

The plane was immense, I'm not sure now what it was - an 'A' something or other - because that sort of thing fails to interest me, but I reckoned there were at least seventy passengers in the cabin.

I'd frequently contemplated life and death. I had vague impressions of Heaven and Hell without actually believing in either but now I have a suggestion.

Here are some estimations which I made to while away flight time. I tried to estimate the total volume of a Business Class cabin on the plane in which I was flying but I couldn't work it out quickly, so I gave up. But let's say the average volume of flatulent gas per person in eight hours is 250mls then in eight hours of flight seventy passengers would produce around eighteen litres of the stuff. Let's add another two litres of belch gas and we come up with twenty litres. I realise that there is an air-conditioning system on an airplane but when one thinks about it...one is trapped in a metal tube with inferior food and seventy-plus other people, thirty thousand feet above sea level and moving at close to the speed of sound in a flatulence filled environment with beds that go flat but are still uncomfortable, this for eight to sixteen hours.

I'd say that was Hell.

I used to smoke, though I didn't at that time, hadn't for thirty years but I think flying was a happier experience when lots of people smoked. The air conditioning on a plane was much stronger. Had to be. I remember being on a Qantas flight from San Francisco (I think) to Sydney. I'd been on a business trip to New York and had stopped off to visit some friends. It was at the time when they had a smoking section - at least in 'Economy' they did - and I was seated at the front of the section in the non-smoking area. I'd intended not to smoke on the trip, so I'd requested that area. Anyway, I changed my mind in the early hours of the morning, Australian time, and walked back to the smoking section in order to satisfy my craving. I think at one time, maybe up until the sixties or even seventies you could smoke anywhere. Maybe I'm wrong. As I passed the other passengers, I noticed that those in the non-smoking section were asleep or looking extremely miserable but as I approached the smoke-hazed smoking section the atmosphere changed and I stepped into a different world of cigarettes, alcohol and general bonhomie. The change was incredible. People, male and female, were standing in the aisle, laughing, joking, lost in intense

conversation or simply relaxing, oblivious to their current locked-in-an-aluminium-tube-careering-through-space
situation. There was happiness, there was calm, and there was friendship.

Things don't always change for the better!

But I digress.

At Dallas, I hired the smallest car I could find. The car was a Vauxhall, for which the car hire woman insisted on using the French pronunciation and drove the four hours to Houston on the Interstate 45. I booked on the next available flight to New York. The *actual* next flight was about to leave and anyway it was full, so I checked into an airport hotel for the night and the following morning flew to New York.

From the airport, I rang the number Tom had given me. A male with a very heavy Hispanic accent gave me an address and phone number in Winnipeg.

I left ten thousand Australian dollars or, at least, the U.S. equivalent at the reception desk of a designated hotel, packaged in a padded envelope for Tom to collect. I hadn't read the report of the dead man on the carousel at Sydney Airport yet. I assumed later that this might have been Tom, but I've always been a 'man of honour' as far as agreements and deals were concerned. The murdered blond-haired man might not have been Tom. I could not and would not take chances. Either Tom was alive, in which case he'd collect the money, or he was dead, in which case he wouldn't. If the latter situation was the case, then the package would languish at the hotel's reception desk for some time until, eventually it would be 'taken' by a receptionist (and good luck to him or her!) or it might be handed in to the police - in which case a corrupt cop would take the money for himself - or herself - or pass it in for addition to general finances or perhaps donate it to charity. Whatever the final destination it was of absolutely no concern to me. I would be dead.

Next, I took a taxi to Penn Station where I booked a reservation on an Amtrak Maple Leaf train to Buffalo leaving the following day. I checked into the Renaissance Hotel for the night. Everything had gone without a hitch, and I felt quite proud of myself, so I ordered the most expensive steak on the room service menu with an equally expensive bottle of Californian Zinfandel and relaxed.

The following day I boarded the train for Buffalo and experienced a quite scenic journey, dozing off at regular intervals.

The reasons I finished my train journey in Buffalo were several. Firstly I'd never seen Niagara Falls, which is easily accessible from Buffalo and the city had been recommended to me by a Canadian I'd met some years ago as an attractive place with some history and some excellent restaurants. The main reason, though, was simply that I wanted to break my journey in case I was being followed. I work on the principle that the more complicated the quarry's journey, the more difficult it will be for the pursuer.

My informant was correct with regard to the city itself; some excellent architecture, but I failed to be impressed with the restaurants. There seems to be a feeling in the United States (in my humble opinion) that good food is directly proportional to the quantity on the plate. There seems too to be a lack of skill in the use of herbs, or 'erbs' as they call them. Again, more is better. By this I mean that the more herb species one uses, the better, they think, will be the taste. A visit to Lyon in France would do most American chefs a great deal of good.

To give the Buffalo-ese their due, though, they are extremely friendly and more than helpful. I liked them a lot.

Two days later I boarded a coach to Toronto.

Big mistake!

Chapter Thirty-five   A Poor Decision

The seating on the coach, a single decker, was comfortable and I was pleased to discover that nobody had been booked into the seat next to mine, so I could stretch out a bit. I was pleased too that the journey would be mercifully short, just over three hours.

In front of me was another seat occupied by a single passenger who, I'd noticed as I got on the coach, was looking unwell, pale and sweaty. I hoped that whatever it was he had, he'd keep to himself and would not infect me.

As it turned out, what he had was a large pistol and after about half an hour into the journey, after the Customs check and the bridge crossing and well into Canadian territory, my neighbour had stood up and walked to the front of the vehicle by the driver.

He said something to the driver who passed him the microphone he had used to welcome us aboard.

We had gone through Customs checks without incident. The guy seated in front of me, who was now by the side of our driver seemed to have no problem. He was a Canadian citizen returning home after a 'few days' in New York. The Customs officer had asked him about his state of health to which he had replied that he thought he was sickening for the 'flu. The Customs officer had nodded but said no more as he moved on to the next traveller, which was me. My Australian passport had attracted some comment and the officer had asked me if I knew of somewhere or other in the Dandenongs because that was where his sister lived. I said that I wasn't familiar with the place since it was in Victoria and I lived in Sydney, which was in the State of New South Wales. I told him that the Dandenong ranges were by reputation quite beautiful, and he confirmed this by telling me that his sister had sent some photographs. He wished me a pleasant stay in Canada and moved on.

The pale one tapped the microphone. The taps were heard quite clearly but he was plainly unused to amplification equipment and next performed the classic 'roadies' confirmation of, "Two, two, two, one, two, one, two!!!"

"Now," said my erstwhile neighbour, who still looked unwell, "this is a hijack!"

A drunken soul at the back of the coach shouted, "Shurrup 'n siddown, ya cocksucker!" at which point and seemingly by way of direct response, the hijacker pointed his pistol at a front seat passenger and shot him.

"For fuck's sake!" whispered the slightly less drunk friend of the voluble one, "Shurrup! Doan annoy the cunt!"

"Jesus Christ!" screamed the woman in the front seat, sitting next to her possibly dead partner. The hijacker remained calm, but the drunk persisted with, "What he do? He shot some poor bastard?" This he exclaimed loudly which caused the hijacker to stare intently at the back seats. There was a sound like that of a fist hitting a slack jaw, which, in fact, was the sound of a fist hitting a slack jaw, the fist belonging to the less drunken friend of his more drunken companion, the slack jaw belonging to the latter. The more drunken soul was not heard from again.

It's strange when it happens. What I mean by this is that everybody and I mean *everybody* has imagined themselves experiencing a hijack. I'd put money on it, big money. Most people, I suspect, would see themselves staying quiet and making themselves as least conspicuous as possible. Others would, Walter-Mitty-like, imagine themselves 'having a go'.

In my case, though I think the impression I've given is one of timidity, my daydreams claimed that faced with the situation, I would 'have a go' and further, would successfully overpower the hijacker to save myself and my fellow passengers. There was always the worry that I would not be quick enough in inspiring others to assist me, but in the end, I would succeed!

But what was the reality?

I was surprised and concerned to discover that my immediate reaction was to plan the best way to overcome the hijacker and I started to look at those that I could see, in an attempt to assess those willing to help. This was definitely a 'modus' that Mando Oliver - or at least 'Castro Mulligan' - would have employed.

Then I realised that while success at saving the current situation would be satisfying, the last thing I needed was publicity. I was, after all, 'on the run' and such heroism would doubtless be reported nationally as well as in Australia, the United States and around the World. Photographs of the 'hero' would be included in the story together with the location of the incident.

Still, I had to assume that my pursuer was still in the United States, perhaps even back in Australia awaiting what he would see as my certain return. I would, I thought, have time to enact the fantasy, accept the praise and adoration that accompanies heroism and still carry out my intended self-killing. I don't like to use the term 'suicide'.

I would confront the hijacker.

I shouted out, "What do you want?"

And he answered, "My brother's freedom".

"Where's your brother?" shouted someone else, whom I felt was intruding on my heroism.

"In Saint Quentin", yelled the hijacker, "for somethin' he ain't done".

"Do you think the authorities in the U.S. are going to let him go?" I asked.

"Yes."

"They might do if you agree to release us all, but they'll chase after the both of you and you'll both finish up in the 'Big House'". I used the term 'Big House', then I thought that perhaps it wasn't in current usage. No matter.

"Let me come up there and I'll show you something that'll help," I said.

"What can *you* show me?" he asked.

"Well, not exactly show but tell you something that'll help but I'm not going to shout it out so's these other passengers can hear."

"What can *you* tell me that'll help? You think I'm stupid, or what?" he asked.

I really *did* think he was stupid, but I said, "O.K., I don't give a rat's arse. Work it out for yourself". And with that I relaxed back into my seat and looked out of the window.

There was a pause, a couple of minutes, maybe less when nothing further was said.

I was suddenly aware of police sirens. Someone must have raised the alarm, perhaps the driver.

Then I heard, quite loudly over the speakers, "O.K.! Mr Smartass, come on up. I'll hear ya but keep both arms in the air. No tricks else you and somebody else will be dead".

As I rose from my seat, I called out, "You won't regret it".

I walked up the aisle of the bus and noticed a strong smell of urine coming from one of the seats. This I ignored and seconds later I found myself next to the hijacker, my arms in the air and what I perceived to be a Glock nine-millimetre semi-automatic pistol pointing at my stomach.

This was a good sign. It meant that the hijacker did not have the pistol in his line of sight. I'd noticed that he had pushed the safety catch into the 'off' position before shooting the unfortunate passenger. He had not touched the safety catch since but maybe...

I'd become interested in or perhaps obsessed with safety catches since my recent experience with Steve Collins.

I leant forward and whispered into his ear, "First off, I'd really appreciate it if you moved the barrel of your pistol away from my body, thanks". He did not move the weapon.

"By the way", I said, "My name's Anton Walczak and I'm on the run." My name, as you know, is not Anton Walczak.

The hijacker's eyes flickered.

"What should I call you?" I asked.

"Peter."

"Peter who?"

"Just Peter."

"Well, 'Just Peter', let me start by giving you a little bit of advice."

"Which is?"

"Which is, I saw you release the 'safety' before you shot the bastard in the front row."

"So?"

"So…you put it back on again afterwards."

"I…"

"Take the fucking catch off again else you're no danger to anyone!"

The hijacker, Peter, looked confused, then after some seconds he looked down and I hit him hard, with my fist clenched, on the left temple. He went down firing the pistol, three shots, the bullets, fortunately, missing all the passengers, except me. I caught one, though luckily it only grazed my calf.

I hit him again…and again, and again, and again until he lay still, and the pistol had fallen from his grasp.

The driver brought the bus to a sudden stop, and we were immediately surrounded by flashing police lights.

A guy in the second row leapt up, saying, "I do martial arts!" The hijacker was face down but just in the process of changing his position to who knew what? The 'martial artist' grabbed the left leg of the hijacker, bent it at the knee and laid the tibiofibula behind the knee of the right leg. He quickly bent the right leg over the calf of the other leg and produced a piercing scream from the hijacker. My assistant released the pressure and the screaming stopped.

"Oh, fuckin' Jesus, I won't move, don't do that again…*please!*"

The hijack was over.

The driver activated the door mechanism and the police, who had clearly seen everything, piled in, disappointment on many of their faces. The potential for 'action' had gone.

We were commanded to remain in our seats. I had sat down in a spare seat at the front, while the shot passenger and his wife were removed - the guy was injured but alive - along with the hijacker who was placed by two police officers into a waiting ambulance and whisked away.

"Well done, fella!" said one of the cops as he clapped me on the shoulder. "You're a hero! That took a lot of guts. We know this guy. Claims to have a brother in jail somewhere, right? Hasn't got a brother…or a brain! Dangerous though. This'll put him away for some years".

"How's the passenger he shot?" I asked.

"He's O.K. Lost some blood but he's O.K. The medics have got him. He'll be O.K. What the fuck did you say to the guy?"

"Just bullshit. Just enough to distract him while I took a whack at him."

"Well it took a lot of guts! You're a hero! Here's the Press. Good luck!"

And with that all I can remember is the flash of cameras.

Chapter Thirty-six   Reflecting at Leisure

My 'heroism' was really stupid. The whole concept of travelling to Toronto by coach had seemed harmless. It did leave me vulnerable, but not in the way expected.

The real disaster was the fact that publicity cannot be avoided. If the news media, newspapers or television, see a story they'll milk it until it's dead. I suppose you can't blame them, it's their job. That's the kind of thing that justifies their existence.

In most cases, of course, publicity is welcomed by the protagonists but in my case…?

What had happened, the hijacking, was not my fault or indeed my responsibility but the heroism could be totally 'sheeted down' to me.

All that I could do was to hope that nobody would see the reports. By that I mean nobody with any relationship to my current activities.

My actions could not be undone. 'The moving finger writes and having writ etc.'

'Castro Mulligan' would not have been pleased.

There's a saying that goes, something like, 'Act in haste, reflect at leisure'. Well, now I was doing a lot of reflecting at a great deal of leisure.

Under normal circumstances, I would have been proud of my actions, amazed but proud. I would have played up the interviews to the hilt. But these were not 'normal circumstances'. I had been responsible for hiring an accomplice to kidnapping, I had been responsible, if unintentionally, for the death of another human being and was being chased across continents by a 'hitman'. The very last thing I wanted was to be identified, let alone identified in a specific location.

In the first few days I got messages on my mobile phone, which said, for example: "What a man! Congratulations! Enjoy the rest of your holiday(?) in Canada. All the best, Tom Granger" and the Tom Granger in question and his fellow SMS writers were messaging from Australia. One old business acquaintance even sent me a photograph of the headlines on the front page of the Daily Telegraph which said, in letters seemingly three feet high "AUSSIE HIJACK HERO SAVES THE DAY (TRIP)" and below that was a photograph of me looking embarrassed, which indeed I was.

Inside, on page three was a full-page spread reporting 'verbatim' an interview I'd had with the New York Times Canadian correspondent, which outlined what had happened together with my 'thoughts and emotions' during my 'terrifying ordeal'. Frankly, I don't even remember giving the interview. As to what I said...

Why had I done it? I suppose I'd done it out of a desire for self-preservation. I think I saw the situation as getting in the way of my intentions, which were to get to Lake Manitoba and to kill myself. Maybe nobody else would have tried. Maybe the hijacker would have shot himself or let everybody go but maybe he'd have been insane enough to kill all the passengers. Maybe he'd had explosives.

Whatever the truth, my cover was completely 'blown' and I had to think fast.

The coach was declared a 'crime scene' and after interminable questioning and statement-taking, replacement vehicles were called up to transport the survivors to Toronto. As the 'hero' I was allocated what could only be described as a limousine with a uniformed driver.

At the Toronto Hotel I was greeted by what seemed to be the entire staff. I was checked in to the most expensive suite and told that a table at the hotel restaurant had been reserved for me and that I should regard accommodation and all other expenses (within *reason*!) as complimentary.

More photographs and another interview for the hotel chain's newsletter ensued.

I had to get away and this I did by means of a judicious payment to the concierge. I told him that I was having problems with a woman in Buffalo and my wife had found out about the affair. I was supposed to be in Europe on business and I needed to get there as quickly as possible to establish some alibis. A couple of thousand dollars got me his services in obtaining a Business Class seat from Toronto to London the following day. The concierge had asked me how I would explain the coverage in the Press and on TV. I explained that we lived deep in country Australia and that my wife never read the papers and we had no TV.

I had to go via New York but that was of no consequence.

What *was* of consequence however was that outside the arrival hall at London Heathrow I saw Mr Black Hat sitting quietly at a café table with a newspaper and a cup of coffee. He didn't look up and ostensibly didn't see me. But I didn't believe that.

I took a taxi into Central London, calmly. Mando Oliver in his role as 'Castro Mulligan' would have remained calm like that.

Chapter Thirty-seven   Backgrounds Poorly Surmised

I now knew that Mr Black Hat was someone called Kevin 'Handyman' Thompson and that he had earned his sobriquet by being the most willing member of the Collins crime syndicate to undertake whatever 'jobs' were available, no matter how dangerous.

So he wasn't an Arab or an Italian and his name suggested his antecedents were probably Anglo Saxon or (Kevin?) Celtic.

Now, for years I'd been inventing a background for various people I wasn't sure about. I did it for Mike Brotchie. Why was he like he was? I hypothesised that he had had a less than loving family life, a weak mother and a dominant father who had likely been violent. I invented two brothers for Mike, one older and one younger, both much taller than him, one a College Football star, the other an academic type destined for high political office. Mike had been a nondescript child with low school grades and a dislike for any sort of physical activity. His father didn't like him and saw to it that the mother withheld any expression of what little affection she had for him

Mike Brotchie's adult character was therefore pre-ordained by his unloving upbringing as the very short, unsporting and un-academic middle son of the family. His bullying, near sadistic approach towards his fellow employees, particularly those whom he considered his inferiors, could be explained by his early family life.

Some years later, my psychological powers were called into serious question! I was in New York on a business trip and rang Tom Klemstein who had long since left Comptex. He told me that he'd been invited to a Christmas party at the Brotchies a couple of years back and had met the short-arsed prick's parents. Apparently, Mike had been their only child and they had worshipped him with all their being. Still did.

But Kevin 'Handyman' Thompson was a different enigma. His swarthy appearance belied his name.

So here's what I came up with: Kevin was the son of a slightly 'bent' Aussie bloke of Irish extraction who'd married a Lebanese girl. That would explain his swarthy complexion and also his Irish Christian name.

I checked the most popular surnames of Ireland list and found, to my surprise, that Thompson came in around number forty-two, well above Donnelly or O'Shea or Kavanagh for example.

So, then I gave him a couple of siblings and an upbringing in North Queensland.

Well, this turned out to be quite inaccurate, as you shall see.

After Kevin Thompson I stopped inventing people's backgrounds. In truth, I was poor at the pastime.

Chapter Thirty-eight   Preparation for my Demise

I was exhausted. The travelling and the mental tension of being followed were taking their toll.

I suspected that Mr Black Hat, or Kevin 'Handyman' Thompson had some sort of computer access to the passenger lists of the major airlines. So I booked three flights: London to Manchester, Manchester to Sydney and London to Toronto. I took the London to Manchester flight then took the train from Manchester to Euston Station, London, then a taxi to Heathrow and a four-hour wait in the First-Class lounge before boarding the Toronto flight. All in all an expensive exercise but under the circumstances, I thought well advised.

Despite having quite a lot of money due to my parsimonious approach to life and some fortuitous property investments, I was still frugal, some would say 'miserly'. My total assets, including my own house, amounted to more than six million Australian Dollars, nevertheless it hurt me to pay out the cash for Business or First-Class seats, even if they *were* necessary. I needed to be comfortable in my travel and saw advantage in the quicker processing that 'Business' or 'First' provided.

I suppose it was my upbringing. My family wasn't poor by any means, at least by the standards of the times, but they were times with uncertain futures. 'Frugality' was the watchword.

I seemed to be mean with myself but with other people, when I met them, which was rarely, I was very generous. Was that because I was a generous person or was it because I liked to appear rich? I wasn't sure.

I took a taxi from Toronto Pearson International to the hotel, this time, the Radisson Admiral on the waterfront. It was here that I happened upon the report of the murder and subsequent carousel ride of the person who might have been Tom. I hoped it wasn't, Tom was a top guy, ignoring for the moment his homosexuality, which had turned out to be only fifty per cent of his sex life anyway, according to him at least. Frankly, I don't like poofters much. It's not the fact that they like people of their own sex - I don't suppose they can help that, it's the way they were born - but I really don't like what they do. If, for example, I see two men even kissing each other, I feel physically sick. Well, maybe that's wrong but that's what happens. Anyway, I could argue that that was the way *I* was born. I did like Tom though. He was a top guy, and he changed my attitude a bit.

I checked into a nice room and relaxed. Room service wasn't bad. In fact, it was really good. I stayed in the room until the following morning, but my sleep had been disturbed by my thoughts. I had become unsure as to whether or not I could really kill myself. Could I do it or did I *want* to do it? I felt so alive at present and this, I realised had been caused by the tension that had built up in me from my being followed, sought out, pursued. Frankly, I was enjoying my new role. This was *living*, this was *exciting*, this was *life*, the *real* thing. Gone was the humdrum life I had led for all those years as a salesman. Gone was the striving for 'figures', the struggle to attain budgets, the desire to impress, to play the hero to sales manager, to colleagues, to clients, to family. My whole existence had been pathetic, unmanly, cowardly even. This, the life that I found myself in now was the life, the path I needed to follow, the path of the hunter or the hunted. I would need to consider my position.

At eight a.m. I went down to the restaurant for a buffet breakfast.

I saw a spare table and sat down, then established my ownership with my newspaper and jacket and left my seat to inspect the food on offer.

As I moved towards the buffet, which looked to be excellent, I noticed another spare table, which had on its surface a black short brimmed straw fedora hat. I turned back to my table, picked up my newspaper and jacket and left the restaurant, pausing only to mumble apologies to the cashier and to tell her of my imminent return…which wasn't going to happen.

The hat may not have belonged to my pursuer, but I was taking no chances. I took breakfast in a small café on a back street some way from the hotel.

Later that morning I checked out of the hotel and took a taxi to the Hertz office on Bay Street. It looked much closer on the map than the journey taken by the taxi so perhaps I was 'ripped off'. No matter, it wasn't worth questioning, I had no need for arguments.

I hired a car and set off toward Winnipeg even though I knew the journey would take around twenty-four hours. I had plenty of time and aimed to do the journey in three days, stopping off for the night in Sudbury and Thunder Bay before arriving on the evening of the third day in Winnipeg. I'd booked ahead for a room in Motel 6 in Sudbury and the Holiday Inn in Thunder Bay. In Winnipeg, I'd booked a four-night stay at the Super 8. That, I thought should be long enough for what I needed to do, which was to collect the explosive and set up the detonation equipment, buy a suitable car with a tow bar then a boat and trailer.

I dismissed the option of a private sale, too complex, and chose a 'reputable' car dealer near the airport from whom I bought a RAM 1500ST truck quad-cab with a near-new tow bar. The vehicle was white and seemed in good condition. It was five years old with around 50,000 kilometres 'on the clock'. I think I paid around twenty-five thousand Canadian dollars for it. I realised after the purchase that the distance was probably measured in miles, not kilometres but no matter.

I returned the hire car to the Winnipeg Hertz depot and took a taxi back to the car dealer to pick up the RAM.

I returned to the hotel, parked the truck then walked up to the main entrance and got into a waiting taxi. As the taxi pulled away from the Hotel, I saw a shortish man wearing a black fedora with a small brim, standing right across the road reading a newspaper. He was dressed in a black overcoat. I felt sure that it couldn't be the 'Handyman', but it reminded me that I had to be careful.

I took the taxi to the address that Tom's 'friend' had given me, a timber clad house in dire need of paint. In the front yard were two near identical Cadillacs, both at least twenty years old, both with rusted bodywork, one red, one green. The once, I imagined, green lawn had died to a brown and beige patchwork of dried mud and sand and was dotted with black oil stains. Shaking like a leaf but trying to appear 'cool' - I think I was successful, I was 'channelling' 'Castro Mulligan' - I passed over an envelope containing seven thousand five hundred U.S. dollars - an excellent exchange rate for the recipient but I wanted no arguments. The cash was laboriously counted by my contact and then laboriously counted again, by my contact's wife, who held a Camel cigarette in her mouth during the whole of the counting process. We were sitting in the kitchen of the house which overlooked a backyard of similar appearance to the front one and which also housed an even older Cadillac. Dirty, food encrusted plates and mugs were strewn across tables, chairs and cabinets although the sink itself was remarkably clean and the taps polished. A pile of pizza delivery boxes decorated one corner of the floor and a foul smelling and aging rottweiler dog lay beneath the table.

I was given a heavy package, which I didn't check, thanked the couple, and returned in the waiting taxi to my hotel.

I checked the package in the safety of my room and inside found exactly what I'd paid for; a block of C4 or its equivalent, two detonators and several metres of plastic-coated wire.

On the morning of the fifth day I extended my stay at the Hotel by one night - a bit of a risk but I was sure that I'd find a boat that was suitable. Using the RAM I visited a boat dealer, also near the airport. I was getting used to the Winnipeg topography, at least that between my hotel and the airport.

To my surprise, because I'm usually pretty efficient at that sort of thing, I'd got my lakes mixed up. The lake I'd thought was Lake Manitoba was Lake Winnipeg. The smaller one to the west was Lake Manitoba. All my daydreams had been of the larger lake so Lake Winnipeg it would have to be. That was a 'Castro Mulligan' decision, for sure! *Decisive!*

After a great deal of discussion as to exactly what sort of fishing I intended to do – fortunately, I'd 'boned up' on matters piscatorial in relation to Lakes Winnipeg and Manitoba - I decided to buy a Lund 1650 Rebel XL Sport with a 30HP Honda outboard motor, but then I saw a cheaper, unbranded, flat bottomed 'tinnie' with a sort of half-cabin, that would suit my purpose better. I was a little worried about draft because I understood that Lake Winnipeg was rather shallow, so the flat bottom had merit. A steering wheel would have been a much more convenient proposition than a tiller but that's what my purchase had, a 25 HP outboard and you steered with that. The boat was eighteen and a half feet long. Ideal

My newly acquired boat was duly connected to the tow bar of the RAM 'pick-up', and I made the trip to Lake Winnipeg to work out my final procedures. I thought it best to get some towing experience and, more particularly to develop my skills in reversing. I'd towed boats before in Australia, but I'd never considered myself an expert. Some people are 'naturals' but not me. I usually took two or three 'goes' before I achieved success.

The road from Winnipeg to Manigotagan on Lake Winnipeg is Highway 59 and then PR304. It was a two-and-a-half-hour drive, but it gave me some good opportunities to stop and practise my reversing.

I drove back to Winnipeg convinced that I'd have to go much further north on my final run, which indeed could be 'final'.

I parked the truck and the boat and trailer in the hotel car park but as far from the entrance as possible. Why I decided on that course of action, I have no idea, but I seemed to have become highly security conscious, doubtless due to the paranoia induced in me by 'the Handyman'.

I returned to my room and ordered 'room service', this time a rather good seafood risotto and a bottle of Californian red. Zinfandel again, I seem to remember.

In the morning I would check out and be on my way.

Chapter Thirty-nine   My Destination. Doubts Continue.

I had calculated that if I wanted to be 'on the water' by early evening I'd need to leave Winnipeg by eight a.m. at the latest. I had a long journey ahead of me, six or seven hours maybe more allowing for stops and the possibility of not finding a suitable launching spot quickly. Manigotagan is relatively close to Winnipeg, but I needed to drive further, possibly much further.

I'd gone to sleep quite early, around ten o'clock, but woke at two the following morning and stayed awake for the rest of the night. What had kept me awake were my current doubts regarding the advisability of my third project, my suicide. One part of me - my intellect I suppose - said that my intention was good, 'noble' even, whilst my heart told me otherwise. The longer I existed in this almost make-believe world, the more I enjoyed it. I had never been happier.

I checked out of the hotel and was on my way at half past seven.

There was some bad weather forecast but not too bad, just some rain and wind from the northeast at 30 knots maximum; all to be expected in early October, nothing to worry about. Actually, it suited my purpose very well because it would discourage most people from going out fishing or just motoring about.

I drove and I thought.

I stopped just short of Manigotagan and went into a café and general store. The establishment sold fishing gear, rods, reels, bait etc as well as general provisions and apart from two staff I was the only one there. I bought a coffee and a cake and sat in the window.

I left the café after having confirmed my presence with the staff by introducing myself by name and asking a few local questions - main fish around the area, local accommodation, that sort of stuff - and left my open wallet on the counter. I was outside before I heard the call from the café manager and had the wallet returned. He would certainly remember me, and I hoped would have read the name on my Australian driver's licence.

Why did I need to be remembered? I'm a helpful sort of a person and my aim was to finish my life spectacularly but without inconvenience to others. If all went according to plan, there would be no identifiable body or debris and I had no desire to take up the valuable time of the police in identifying me. I suppose I could have left a note at the launch point, wherever the Hell that was going to be, but I thought that would have been a bit too dramatic.

Just south of Loon Straits, the wind came up and I thought it might be wise to check the boat for any loose items. There had been a kind of camping cover supplied with the boat or it might simply have been a cover to keep snow out during the winter months when the temperature was low, and this cover was lying at the bottom of the boat. I felt I should secure it.

I stopped the car and went back to the boat where I decided to fold the cover up and stow it beneath the roof of the half-cabin, though it had a scant claim to that description, being simply a roof under which one could shelter from the elements.

I pulled the cover out of the boat in order to fold it and to my horror saw a body, lying prone, a neat hole in its forehead. The body was that of my friend 'St Anthony'!

Poor Tony. It immediately dawned on me that he'd read of my 'heroism' in the Australian Press and had been on a mission to save me from myself. He'd certainly reacted quickly.

He'd reckoned without the 'Handyman'.

I'd seen very few cars on the road, and I seemed to be alone. With considerable difficulty, I removed my dead friend and dragged him behind a small hillock. This may seem a very uncaring thing to do but I'd considered the situation carefully. Tony was dead and his mortal remains were inanimate. That was what I'd thought then. It was, rightly or wrongly, the end for my friend and no sympathy or remorse or care could bring him back. Besides, I myself was on my way to my doom.

Or maybe I wasn't!

I found myself looking down on the peaceful body of Tony and saying a prayer. Incredible, knowing my attitudes at the time but there remained somewhere in the deepest recesses of my brain some vestiges of religious thought, residual from my childhood, despite my non-faith-based upbringing. I suspect I'm not alone in experiencing such feelings.

I left Tony and continued my journey.

Some way North of Loon Straits I felt exhausted. It was past three o'clock and the Canadian autumn darkness was not far away. On a whim, I turned off the road and followed the track down to the lake's shore. I couldn't believe it! Here was the perfect location for what I was about to do; a worn concrete ramp with a decrepit timber structure along one side and nobody about. To tell the truth no one in their right mind, except perhaps the keenest of fishermen, would be 'about' at this time of the year. It was cold and rainy and thoroughly miserable. Snow would soon arrive, I supposed.

I reversed down the ramp and slid the boat off the trailer into the water (Christ, the water was cold!) I reversed the boat so that it pointed away from the shore and secured it to the single bollard on the primitive timber 'jetty' at the side of the ramp. I secured the boat with my 'grandfather's knot' to the cleat on the boat's port gunwale. My intention now was to take the boat out, stay on the water all night - I had enough clothing to make this possible - have some food and wine and then make my final decision.

My 'final decision'? For a while now I'd realised that I was enjoying my life immensely. Life had become exciting. Would I end my life in anticipation of something that might never happen, or would I wait until it did? Would I return to shore and continue my 'new' life? We would see!

I returned to the car and drove about half a kilometre down the road to a stand of pines into which I drove and parked the car. I walked back to the ramp, noting that both car and trailer were invisible from the road. It would probably be quite a long time before my vehicle was discovered, not that it would matter if all went well with my plans, but I wanted to make identification easy but not *too* easy. Why? Well I certainly don't have an answer to that question. You do some unexpected things when one of the options is to kill yourself. As I approached the ramp again – it was getting dark now - I saw that there was a large car parked a way off to one side. I had not seen this vehicle at the time of launching my boat. Maybe it was there, maybe it wasn't. Somehow, I didn't think it was but it was black so it might not have registered with me. The car seemed empty so it might have been parked there for some time or perhaps it had passed me when I was hiding my car and trailer. Perhaps the driver had gone out fishing earlier. I would have to look out for him.

Then I looked toward my boat and was consumed with fear. Someone was sitting amidships, his back towards me and that someone was wearing a black overcoat and a small-brimmed black straw fedora hat. He, it was a man, sported a black scarf looped fashionably around his neck.

And then that somebody called my name. I walked up to the jetty and climbed onto it, approaching the boat. The lone occupant was Mr Black Hat and in his hand was a very large pistol.

Chapter Forty   End Game

"Come and join me," said Mr Black Hat, "You want a drink?"

"Why not?" I said, getting into the boat with a great deal of faked bravado.

What would 'Castro' have done?

"I've got a flask of tea and some ginger nuts, or the Canadian equivalent", he said.

I'd expected something stronger but at least I was still alive.

Mr Black Hat's shoes were totally unsuitable for the harsh Manitoba environment; expensive black leather slip-ons with an imitation gold buckle. The last time I'd had a really positive sighting of both him and his hat had been from the café opposite the Sydney apartments over two weeks ago. But I knew now that I'd 'seen' him several times since then. I felt my heart race. How had he managed to track me down?

"Hi!" he said. "Let me introduce myself. I'm Kevin. Surprised to see me, I expect."

"In a way, yes," I bluffed, "who *are* you? Have we met?"

"Did you do the killing?"

"Killing? What killing?" I lamely replied, "I really don't know what..."

"Let us not be stupid."

"No," I said, with scant conviction. "No!" I said again, "I don't know anything about...a *killing*, did you say?"

"Bullshit...O.K., we can do this the easy way or the hard way. Let's say, for the sake of argument you didn't do the killing, who did? Who then?" He poured the tea from a huge flask and asked "Milk?'

"Yes, thanks, just a touch."

"Sugar?"

"No, thanks."

He splashed some milk into the plastic cup and passed it to me.

"Look, mate, er…" I said, "I'm here for the fishing, walleye, carp, pike in particular, maybe sturgeon. I'm hoping for a sturgeon, you never know. Soft plastics and…"

"O.K.," said Kevin, "Last chance, then it's the hard way. Who killed Collins? Biscuit?" He offered the packet.

"Er, thanks, yes, thank you." I paused; it was pointless bluffing further. "The gay guy," I said.

"No, he didn't," said Mr Kevin Black Hat, "You did. Did you intend to kill him?"

"No."

"You shot a hole through his nose."

"An accident."

"Painful."

"Yes."

"He died of a heart attack."

"Yes."

"Why did you shoot into his kneecaps *after* he'd died?"

"I don't know. What are you going to do?"

"After he'd *died*? Very brave, very brave, *very* brave."

"I'm not proud of that and why I did it, I don't know. I wish now that I hadn't. What are you going to do?" My terror was mounting, my throat becoming constricted, my mouth dry.

"My assignment is to find you and kill you, making sure you know you're going to die and making sure you know who's responsible."

"How did you…er…find me?"

"Tracking devices on your luggage, on the hire car you used, on the one back there you bought, asking questions, posing as private investigators, posing as police, having, shall we say, access to certain lists? Asking questions mainly."

"There were more? Than you, I mean", I asked.

"Just three but me mainly. It wasn't hard."

"Collins is dead…your boss. Who's giving the orders now?"

"There's always somebody. There's no stated line of succession. Somebody's always in the wings, but nobody had Steve's Emperor Martyr. It just happens and everybody accepts it. Them as don't..."

"It's actually..."

"Yeah, smartarse, I know what it is...*actually*. It was a joke."

"Oh! Funny."

"Thanks. You're going fishing?"

"Yes."

"No, you're not. No rods."

"Handlines."

"Bullshit! No handlines either. Why are you going out?"

"Will you let me go out if I promise to come back?"

"No."

He raised his right arm. Rotating his hand. I heard a car door open and looked toward the black Cadillac. The rear door of the vehicle was open, and a large figure exited the car. The figure walked towards us. I recognised the figure as soon as he was within ten yards of us. My heart raced.

"Did you really need to kill Tony...my friend?" I asked.

"Actually, I did. He was getting in the way. Asking too many questions."

"Couldn't you just have, I don't know...dissuaded him?"

"No. No time!"

"Do I detect a Yorkshire accent? Slight?"

"You're not very good at accents, are you?"

"Well, north of England?"

"A few miles north of Yorkshire."

"Geordie?"

Mr Black Hat looked exasperated. He said, "Fuck off."

"Where then?"

"Cumberland. Dad was a farmer. I was earmarked to be one too, but Mum and Dad joined a nutty church, 'Exclusive Brethren'. I bailed out, joined the 'Merchant'. Jumped ship in

Darwin. Came south. Bookie's runner amongst other things, for two years then worked for Mr Collins, doin' odd jobs. Never looked back. You know Clarrie? Yes, of course, you do. Clarrie?"

"Yes," said Baskerfield, "I know Mr Brooks fulsome well. Mr Brooks was responsible for a great deal of inconvenience on my part and, may I say, without intending the giving of any offence, considerable embarrassment in the premises of not a few financial establishments in Her Majesty's capital city".

"Oh, yes! You may, Mr Baskerfield, you may, you may certainly say that."

Somewhat emboldened, though for what reason I didn't know, I asked, "Why are we holding a conversation in Dickensian English?"

"We're being ironic," said Baskerfield, pronouncing the first two syllables of that word as 'iron'...as in the song 'Any Old Iron'.

"It's i*ron*ic," I said, "one pronounces the 'r'"

Baskerfield looked confused but then said, "Hit him, Kev, hit the cunt".

"Glad to oblige!" He did as bid, using my face as a target and the back of his hand as the weapon. It was painful, tears sprang to my eyes. There was a heavy ring on the middle finger of the 'hitting hand' and this had made a visible impression on the upper region of my cheek.

"You see," said Kevin, I'd already embarked on some research prior to your disappearance. You remember Anita Sutton?" I nodded, "Of course you do. You deceived her at the very least, after her poor daughter died. She drowned apparently. Bit simple, she was. You know what Brooksie? Not so sure it was accidental, if you get my drift. Certainly unlikely to have been suicide. Happy girl by all accounts. Bit of...help? Perhaps?"

The 'Handyman' paused as if musing, "Then, your friend Mr. Baskerfield contacted me. He told me that he'd been taken for a mug...well, not entirely true, that's unfair, let's say 'taken advantage of', 'made to feel foolish', 'inconvenienced considerably'. First mistake, yours; Clarence knew the travel agent you used and…well a bit of persuasion here and a bit there and before we knew it," he smiled, "we'd got your whole itinerary".

Then he said, "Why're you here?"

"O.K., here's the truth. I'm going to kill myself."

"Bullshit. How?"

"Explosives. I'm going to get serious cancer. I know it. It runs in the family. I'm going to pre-empt my death from cancer. I'm going to pre-empt the pain."

"Actually," said Baskerfield, still standing on the jetty, "*we're* going to kill you, though a lot slower than you could ever imagine, so pain won't be pre-empted. I can assure you of that. The process involves rope, knots, water…very cold…and knives. See if you can guess what the process is. See if you can work it out. See if you can, Mr Brooks."

"Did you bring the rope?" asked Kevin.

"In the boot."

"Go and get it."

" 'kay."

Clarrie walked back toward the car, and I realised that my one and only chance of escape would arise pretty much as soon as he concentrated on opening the trunk of the car. His hands would be occupied, and his entire body would be geared to locating the rope. Little enough delay before he'd spring into action but 'little enough' was good enough for me, and no more than I could have hoped for.

"I really did intend to kill myself", I said.

"Bullshit."

I'd formulated a plan of escape as I'd sat there in terror. There was a heavy spanner sitting atop the explosives and if I could get to it quickly enough and be in a position to swing it with some degree of accuracy at Mr Black Hat's head, I'd have a faint chance of escape. The only worry I had was that I might have omitted to use my grandfather's 'cowboy knot' on the rope tying the boat to the jetty. I thought I had but now I wasn't sure. If there was a delay in releasing my vessel from its mooring, disaster would ensue. I thought I'd used the knot, although now I couldn't for the life of me remember which end, the boat end or the jetty end.

I should describe the knot. My grandfather was American, my mother's dad, and he always claimed that he'd been a Sheriff's deputy in a town in Texas. He showed me this knot which he claimed was that used by all the lawmen in the 'old days' to tie their horses to the hitching rails. It involved the use of a sort of slipknot and allowed for a quick departure from saloons, bars and roadhouses. I always made use of this knot although I'd never had the need of a 'quick escape'…until now!

"Have a look in that box under the covered section. You'll see. I'll show you."

I partially pulled the box out from under the forward deck - out a little from the 'half-cabin' - removed the lid and showed the explosive and its means of detonation.

"Jesus!" he said and stood up for a closer look. He was unbalanced and I picked up the heavy spanner, which lay on the explosives box and swung it at his head. I was never athletic, never accurate with bat or ball and I barely caught his scalp before I pushed him overboard. I leapt to the engine and opened the fuel valve, pulled the choke out full then tugged like a demon on the starter cord, which, to my delight, started the engine immediately. Smoke rose thickly from the exhaust.

The 'Handyman's' head was bleeding as he rose in chest deep water and lunged for the boat. I dived to the mooring rope and was thrilled to discover that grandfather's knot had been tied at the boat end on the gunwale cleat. I released the rope and struck out with the spanner again as I pulled away from the ramp. I missed my target completely. Mr Black Hat made a fresh leap at the boat and grabbed hold of the gunwale, which was surprising considering the weight of water that would have soaked into his heavy woollen overcoat. He had lost the pistol. I hit out at his fingers with the spanner and made some minor contact. He roared, floundering in the water as I motored away. I saw him get to his feet and wade with high steps to the shore then run towards the black car. The overcoat must have weighed a ton. He ran to the trunk and ripped open the lid that Baskerfield had just closed. From the trunk he took out another pistol, I could barely see it, but I could sense its shape. The weapon was huge, and I guessed that like the first one, a silencer was attached. I was about a hundred metres from the shore by that time and moving fast. I saw him drop down on one knee and take aim. I ducked below the level of the transom.

A hole appeared with a bang above my head as I heard the muffled report of the pistol from the shoreline. The bullet went, I know not where. I heard another report from the pistol, but no hole appeared. I must have been nearly two hundred metres away from the ramp by now and moving into the gloom of a wet Manitoba evening.

Kevin The Handyman's aim would likely have been hampered by his understandable shivering and the injury to his hand but, in addition, the accuracy of pistols leaves a lot to be desired, especially silenced and at long range. I was, I considered, out of danger. I put my head above the transom and could barely make out the shoreline. Mr Black Hat and his newly acquired friend would, I thought, easily find my car, and wait for my return. They would have a very long wait.

Chapter Forty-one
A Decision then the Decision Reversed

I motored off to my destiny, now changed. I would not kill myself with the explosives I'd acquired. Life had become fun. I would stay with the new life I'd made for myself. I would make mistakes, that was a 'given' but they would be my own mistakes and I'd own them…and laugh at them!

I pondered a while on my failure to realise how quickly Clarrie would have returned to Australia and felt embarrassed in the knowledge that I'd not had the faintest suspicion that he would contact my pursuer, the 'Handyman'.

The waves weren't too bad, no whitecaps that I could see, and the wind seemed to be a steady twenty knots maximum. All seemed to be going well.

I'd brought with me some jumbo shrimp, which we would have called prawns in Australia. The shrimp were 'green' - uncooked that is - and I had with me a gas-fired hotplate. A small gas cylinder had been supplied with the cooking set-up, which had been included in the boat deal. Considering the object of my trip, the shrimp were unnecessary, a bit of an indulgence, I suppose, but what the Hell? I had intended to go out in style and to prove that I also had with me a rather expensive bottle of vintage French Champagne, *Dom Pérignon*, actually. Cost me a lot!

I turned on the gas and fired up the burners under the hotplate.

As the prawns began to sizzle my mind became clear. I was not going to end my life, not now and not until I really had contracted cancer and then not until my condition became terminal. I had begun to enjoy my life, to enjoy the tensions, to enjoy being hunted, to enjoy the evasions. I would stay on the water tonight; I would eat my prawns and drink my champagne. I would sleep, I would wake up with the dawn and then make for the nearest shoreline. Somehow, I would return to my vehicle and somehow, I would escape. I would live and enjoy my new life,

Thirty minutes later, I supposed I was about three kilometres from my launch point. The wind had picked up to over thirty knots and I expected that the whitecaps had started to form although I couldn't see them. It was very dark outside the boat, but my shrimp were starting to sizzle. The boat was starting to rock a bit but by heading fairly slowly into the wind, conditions on board weren't too bad. I opened the champagne and drank a 'glass', a plastic one, in two gulps. Not the best way to savour a good vintage but I had the whole bottle to myself and ahead of me, so I'd savour it more carefully with the shrimp. I turned the shrimp over. They smelled wonderful.

The problem was the water. The wind was picking up and the waves were building

A 'freak' wave hit me broadside and I only just stopped the hotplate from falling over.

Now, I'd always been of the opinion that there was no such thing as a 'freak' wave. It's an expression used by incompetents; people who get washed out to sea or knocked off their surfboards, fishermen who get swept off rocks, people just walking along the rocks under a cliff, people who walk along a beach and suddenly find themselves up to their waists in water, or people in boats that aren't equipped for the conditions. There's always a *reason* for a 'freak' wave.

Well, I'd been hit by such a wave, and I guessed that there must be some explanation for its being produced, maybe an anomaly in the lake floor; an underwater hill or something.

I was thinking about that when the second wave hit; again at an angle to the wind and the swell. This time the boat took on water over the gunwales and the shrimp were washed off the hotplate. One landed on my thigh, and I felt its warmth through my pants, but I was immediately cooled by a third wave which filled the boat. That coupled with the force of the wind under the partially lifted vessel - a flat bottom was not the most suitable hull shape in these conditions - destabilised it enough to turn it over and tip me out

The next wave lifted the boat - and me - and drove us both several metres from where we'd started. I instinctively fought back and managed to hold my position, but the boat was completely overturned and disappeared slowly beneath the waves, several metres away. That wasn't meant to happen. The boat was surely designed not to sink, I was certain there was enough 'flotation'...but maybe the weight of the outboard had dictated otherwise. There had certainly been a 'stern first' component to the sinking.

I thought, incredibly, about my numerous failures: the Sydney Marathon experience and then my failure with what I'd planned for Collins. I remembered my failed burglary and the 'cucumber frame' incident. I thought of my failure to succeed in changing my appearance. I recalled the disappearance of my sexual potency and my stupid heroics on the Toronto bus. Now, this. After all my mental turmoil, after my decision to abandon my plans and live my new life, fate had taken and destroyed my programme, I was about to die from hypothermia and not at all spectacularly.

I was unsure whether to laugh or cry.

I started to cry but then stopped and roared with laughter though with scant conviction. I seemed to have been a failure in everything in which I'd become involved. I was a total clown. I was doomed to die a very cold, quiet and lonely death rather than being blown to 'smithereens' as planned. 'Castro Mulligan' would not have been impressed.

I felt like sobbing again, but I didn't.

I floated for some minutes, the coldness of the water quickly becoming evident. And then I saw it. A humpback whale? Impossible but whatever it was, it rose like one. And then it collapsed back onto the surface, about ten metres away a dark shape, a hump. Was it a whale? Not in a lake, whales live in the sea, but certainly something large. A sturgeon? They're not *that* big. Big 'yes', but not that big and sturgeon were slim fish. Maybe it was a kind of fresh-water dolphin. Not in these northern climes, surely. Was I to be eaten by an unknown sea creature?

Then, I realised what I was looking at and I understood immediately what had happened. The boat had, indeed, sunk and the hot-plate flame had been extinguished but the gas bottle had not been shut off and the propane, or butane or whatever it was had continued to flow and had filled the hull, increasing the buoyancy, until it had risen to the surface.

I was freezing by now, but the situation made me smile. If I could make it to the boat, I might be able to right it. I struck out for the floating hull and could smell the occasional sweet odour of gas on the wind.

As I neared the boat, I realised that what was happening confirmed my theory as to why the boat had re-surfaced. Every so often the hull would lift and with a 'blurt', gas would be released from beneath the submerged gunwale. My explosive device would have left the hull but would have been trapped by the front deck, the cover of the 'half-cabin'. The hotplate and gas bottle had been loosely lashed to one of the cross struts of the hull. The gas was still flowing and increasing buoyancy.

I reached the hull, grabbed hold of the outboard motor, and pulled myself up until I was able to climb on top of the hull. I felt sure that I could 'right' the boat, but it was colder out of the water than in it.

I was just contemplating re-entry, perhaps I'd be able to lift one side of the boat and let the wind assist me in my efforts when the explosion occurred.

I must say that immediately after the explosion, I was astonished to find myself where I find myself now.

I was highly amused by the nature of the explosion and what had led up to it, but it was strange that I was unable to relate my amusement to my mortal self. The body in the water - or at least the parts of the body in the water - seemed to be quite unrelated to my current form and this hasn't changed during the days, weeks, years, aeons I've been here. Nevertheless, I was highly amused because once again, a conclusion had been reached but the conclusion had been different from the one which had been anticipated. My mortal self had died at the hand of fate rather than my own and in fact, the involvement of my own hand had been rejected. I, my mortal self, had decided that death - my own - should be postponed but this had not been the case and it was easy to perceive the similarity of this to the total physical and mental collapse at the end of the Sydney Marathon or the death of Steve Collins with my mortal self's lack of involvement.

Come to think of it, my struggle with ED (as the Medical Profession would abbreviate it) amounted to the same thing, as did my heroics on the Toronto bus and my poor assessment of the judges of the Archibald Prize entries: failure and disappointment following anticipated success.

I'm not a religious person. In fact, I find all religions laughable. How, I ask, can they all be right? Judaism, Islam and I suppose Buddhism are all monotheistic, Christianity too, although it does promote the concept of a Trinity. Hindus tell us there are many gods, the ancient Greeks and the Romans did too, as did the old Scandinavians. It all seems like bullshit to me.

On the other hand, I've never claimed atheism. Maybe there is a God -it's certainly beginning to look like it - a Supreme Being, a Lord of the Universe, perhaps it's just a Supreme Force.

We take for granted everyday things that would have seemed totally impossible to our great, great grandfathers. We accept the nostrums of the medical brother and sisterhood: Thalidomide prescribed for 'Morning Sickness', 'Stress' causing stomach ulcers until the truth is revealed and announced without apology. So why not a God...to be discovered, say, next month?

What I knew, when I'd first arrived, was that I was in 'Phase One' and had the ability to re-create high points in my life and repeat those experiences *ad infinitum* or until I decided they should stop.

I now know that I have progressed to 'Phase Two' and I am to expect something called a 'Gifting' before progressing to the final stage. My impression is that I will be given something I've always dreamt of having, and in my case, it surely had to be an 'AC Cobra', without doubt, the most beautiful sports car ever designed and built. Was it possible that I could get the satisfaction of driving such a car in my present situation? It was never going to be possible for me to have such a car in the 'mortal' world. A 'Shelby Cobra' in original condition with low mileage recently went for over two million dollars.

In 'Phase Two' there was less feeling of physicality. It was more 'dreamlike' but the physical was still possible. I knew, deep down, that I would be receiving an 'AC Cobra' in the 'Gifting' and I gradually got to realise that I would possess the roads on which to drive it. For how long, I had no idea, but I knew that it would be long enough to fully experience the pleasure.

I know everything and yet nobody has told me. There are no 'others' here but I know I'm in 'Phase Two' and that there are three phases.

How do I know?

I didn't see the explosion. How could I? I was still alive, and I had no idea why it had occurred without my physical involvement, perhaps the gas had dried out the contacts until they made...well, *contact.* I felt nothing apart from an instantaneous increase in pressure, but I saw the immediate aftermath. There were bits of boat and bits of me floating about on the surface of the lake, but the majority of the stuff had sunk. Remarkably, a leg, quite naked was floating with a bit of my lower side attached and was that some intestines? Or was it rope from the boat. I couldn't be sure. I think it was rope. And, oh yes, there was my lower jaw and my tongue or maybe it wasn't. Quite fascinating and in some ways distressing, I can admit it now, it was traumatic. I think most of what I saw was in my imagination. I believe now that it was really too dark to see anything.

I tried to see 'Mr Black Hat' and Baskerfield too. What would they be doing? Had they heard the explosion? If not, would they wait for my return? Were they still waiting? Unfortunately, it was impossible to see further than the water directly below. It was as if I was in a kind of bubble of consciousness with visibility limits.

In any event, that's all over now. Hours have passed. Hours? Days maybe. Weeks? Years? Eternities?

I'm looking forward to the 'Cobra'.

I'm totally alone though I'm deliriously happy. I know exactly how things are going to 'pan out'. I seem to get this information somehow, maybe by some kind of osmosis because nobody has spoken to me. I've seen nobody, nor do I want to. There is nobody here. I'm alone. Totally.

My soul will split...this I *do* know (it's part of the knowledge one acquires in stage two)...and will migrate into other beings. I'm acutely aware of who those other beings are. One will be the son of a farmer in the Northeast of England, another will be the son (they're all sons) of an impoverished Hindu in Goa, another born into a patrician family in Boston, Massachusetts, another to an unmarried drug addict in Malmö, Sweden, another, the last one, undecided as yet.

The remainder of my soul will stay with me as I become one with the feelings I've experienced during the early part of my stay. The feelings will become one. They are all similar. *And I will become that feeling!*

But where is the 'Gifting'? It will have to come soon because 'Phase Three' the final stage is fast approaching.

I put my hand up to my mouth and feel to my surprise, that I have a moustache and beard. There are spectacles hooked around my ears. They rest on my nose. I hold the spectacles by the frame. I want to see what they look like, but they seem to be part of my head. Connected. I can't remove them. No matter.

My hair is much longer than before and very thick. There are no mirrors, but I know that it is jet black with some grey sections.

I say, to no one in particular because I'm alone "Do you have a modus, Hanna?" It's what 'Castro Mulligan' would ask in the TV series *Whipsnade*.

So is this the 'Gifting'? I'm sure it is but I'd never considered that possibility. I'd hoped for, imagined, something material, the AC was my bet, but this is what I really wanted. This was perfection. This was my 'Gifting'.

Then I see Hanna, the one from the series. She's blurry, which I know means she's simply a character in a play, not a real person. Still, I ask her, "Do you have a modus?"

"Yes." She replies.

"Will you go via Amsterdam?"

"Yes,"

"Have you considered...?

"Hamburg?"

"Yes."

"Not possible."

"There's no other way?"

"No, Amsterdam is best."

"Then go. Leave tonight. Don't get caught because we'll have to deny everything."

I was Mando Oliver, I was 'Castro Mulligan'!

Hanna kisses me and leaves.

I'll be going into 'Phase Three' soon. This is the final phase where you feel unbelievably happy, and I *will* be going as 'Castro Mulligan'. I'll be happy because I've retained all the joy from the recurring dreams of my most exciting life experiences. That happened in 'Phase One' and to some extent in 'Phase Two'. I know for sure that this is the case. I know too, or I *think* I know, that in 'Phase Three' I'll have no memory, no opinions, no senses, no knowledge, just happiness but I think I'll retain the physical body of 'Castro Mulligan'.

Nobody judges here. Nobody questions your morality, what you did when you were alive. There is no punishment, no purgatory, no Hell, no Devil, maybe no God. Just being. Just happiness. So much for the ridiculous edicts and decrees of religions in the mortal world.

I've arrived at the beginning of 'Phase Three' now. I know it.

I enter...by which I mean I don't actually physically enter anything but, I accept.

But where am I? How did I get to wherever it is I am?

Incredibly, I seem to be in the middle of a stage, a concert stage; there is no proscenium arch, no curtain. I'm alone. There is no audience.

There is some music faintly playing. It's very faint but I'm sure it's *Dirait-on* by Lauridsen, one of my favourite pieces of music.

There are some people coming into the back of the auditorium from both sides and they move into the back row. I haven't seen people here before.

Now more people are arriving. Again, they come in from both sides and meet in the middle. They fill up the second row from the back. Then more people for the third row and more and more until, as they start to get closer, I start to recognise some of the audience. They're not people that were my friends, but I knew them. There's that guy whom I used to see walking and there's old Frank 'What's-his-name' the butcher, Irene Patrick who ran the choir I was in at the time. All dead long ago.

The seats are filling up. They're doing so with tidiness, with precision.

People come in from both sides of the rear of the seating, in good order and they file slowly into each row until they meet in the middle. Then everybody sits down and the process begins again with the next row and so on.

Soon, there remain only three empty rows at the front and in they come. There's my family, all together, my wife, my son, my daughter with Wayne, her 'ex', Frank Hardry, Mike and Eileen Brotchie, for Christ's sake, that fellow Klemstein, the Yank from Comptex, USA, friends and acquaintances I haven't seen in years. Dr Bromwich, my old doctor, he died in an air crash, Kevin Pang, my old dentist. I didn't know he'd died. Lots of people, men and women I knew or who'd had regular contact with me. Oh, look! There's Monty Jacobs! I've known Monty since Primary School although I never socialised with him; maybe once or twice at the pub when I was in my late teens and early twenties. I lost touch with him after he married that silly bitch Angela Romano. Oh, Angela's with him. They're *both* dead?

It suddenly strikes me! These people, these friends, these family members, these acquaintances are at the age I knew them, all of them. I knew that Mike Brotchie had died, and I was glad of it, but his wife Eileen I thought would have been still alive when I died but she looked the same age as when I knew her and that was at about aged thirty-five.

I had changed dentist when I was about fifty and Kevin Pang would have been forty or so then and he must have been alive when I was in my late sixties because I still got 'reminders' from him so he was still alive when he was over sixty but here he was still in his forties.

Time. There is no time here. It's not measured in hours or days or years.

It simply doesn't exist.

That left the front row and who should come in from the right but 'Saint Anthony', Tony Howarth, my best mate? He took the middle seat in the front row and smiled up at me. There was nobody following him, and nobody entered the front row from the other side either. Tony was alone in the front row. Tony died? Yes, of course, he did. I saw him. He raises his right hand to the level of his shoulder and wriggles his fingers. I nod slowly in response.

I feel it inadvisable to move because I'm at 'centre stage' and that's where I need to be. I try to move position slightly but my legs don't seem to work. In fact, I appear to be totally paralysed from the waist down.

The audience is smiling. Some are waving to me, furtively, as though they don't want to seem to be saying, 'I know him! He's a friend of mine!'

The house lights are dimmed then a spotlight illuminates a door, off to the side of the stage, through which appears a stocky man of middle height. He has a rather swarthy face but is very good looking. He is dressed in a well-cut light blue suit beneath which is a tan shirt and a rather 'loud' tie. It is in the shape of a fish. His hair, which is black with some flecks of grey is slicked back with the aid of pomade and he's sporting a pencil thin moustache. On three of the fingers of his right hand he's wearing rings. They seem 'flashy', 'tasteless'. One is heavy, solid gold containing a huge solitaire diamond…or perhaps a zircon, no, I'm sure it's a diamond. He has been 'made-up' as if for a stage play or a television interview. I can see the line on the back of his neck, which shows where the cosmetic ends and his natural skin begins. There is a very light dusting of fine powder on top of the 'make'-up'.

The man has a very strong neck and just above the collar of his shirt at the back I can see evidence of a very thick gold chain. It looks as though he has dressed hurriedly.

He looks Italian, perhaps a politician or a used car salesman.

Overweight. Untrustworthy.

He walks confidently to centre stage and acknowledges the applause from the audience, who are now standing. He thrusts one arm out toward them, fingers outstretched, palm downwards. He lowers his arm, and the audience sits as one. There is a kind of glow above his head.

He begins his speech. It's not in English, it's slightly 'guttural' but it isn't German. It's Arabic, I think. I understand nothing but the audience, some of them my closest friends, *do*. They laugh at the occasional joke. They applaud the occasional statement. Then I recognise a word that's repeated over and over. It's 'Adonai'. Then another word that I know; 'Elohim', then 'Tov'. The language is Hebrew - not an attractive tongue - I've always thought the loveliest was Brazilian Portuguese - I had a girlfriend from Sao Paulo once, just for a short time. The speech finishes and the speaker leaves to palpably emotional applause. Many in the audience have tears running down their cheeks. Some reach out toward the exit through which the speaker has departed as though to restrain him. During the time He was on the stage He did not acknowledge my presence.

I realise that each time I use 'he' or 'him' or 'his' in the relating of my story and in reference to the speaker, the 'h' is being changed to a capital. It's confusing! God looks like that and is *Jewish*? Well, why not? The Old and New Testaments seem to confirm this. But he looks like *that*? He wore white leather shoes and a white belt.

Now the audience members are all talking, in a sort of unison, well, to the same rhythm at least. Maybe it's a prayer, maybe a poem.

The Lauridsen has begun again, softly.

I look up and notice for the first time that there is a balcony running around the auditorium. No, there are two, one above the other. There are people up there too. They look like tradespeople, carpenters, electricians, plumbers all wearing their work clothes, some of it 'Hi-Viz', all with their partners, all looking down at me.

I can't understand why but I suddenly realise that I'm probably there for my singing. When I was in my forties and fifties and even into my sixties I had a fine voice, bass-baritone it was, and I was always selected to solo if it was required in whatever piece we were singing. Yes, I was here for my voice, I was here to sing, and my singing would have become sublime. The talking (or was it chanting?) stops. There is absolute silence. I look to the side of the stage; I don't know why I do that but I suspect that I sense the audience is looking that way.

Then I see another figure. It's a woman, totally naked. She's tall, much taller than me and she seems to be carrying a paddle, a 'stand-up board' paddle or maybe one that would be used in a racing canoe. She must be my duet partner. She *will* be. I bet she's a contralto but why is she naked? And why the paddle? I reach a hand down to my hip. I'm naked too. Why?

Despite this, I feel confident. We will sing together. What will we sing? Something from opera? Yes! I'll choose Rossini. She'll know 'Dunque io son' from *The Barber of Seville*. It's difficult and I've never sung it before, but I know I can cope with it now.

She'll know it.

My hand goes to my beard. My beard is gone, the glasses too. Panicked, I grab at my hair. The thick, black-with-some-streaks-of-grey hair has gone too. I feel my original - my own - hair. I'm unable to check but I know that my sandy hair has returned. I surmise now that I'm naked so that when I look down I can see my body hair, it's sandy ...ginger.

I am no longer Mando Oliver, no longer 'Castro Mulligan'. Was I him, them, for a year? A month? A day? Seconds? Eternity?

I look at the woman, who is walking slowly towards me. She is smiling but what does the smile truly signify? Welcome? Cynicism? Ridicule? Retribution? The smile is terrifying. I think I know the woman.

I know her. It's Annette. Annette my victim, Annette made whole, Annette made healthy, Annette made strong. Annette is beautiful. The Lauridsen stops and it's Carl Orff now. *Oh Fortuna!* Loud. Very loud!

As Annette walks, slowly but insistently towards me I can see what she's carrying. It's not a paddle.

It's an axe. It's a very big axe!

'Oh Fortuna
Velut luna
Statu variabilis
Semper crescis
Aut decrescis'

The lyrics drip with irony.

'Oh Fortune, you are like the moon, waxing and waning!'

I realise now that I've been wrong, that I've had the waxing. Now it will be the waning, but will it be in my power, as it was with the waxing, to stop the repetition? I don't know.

I was wrong. There *is* retribution here.

Annette comes close. She has become very tall. She is magnificent. Statuesque. Sexually indomitable.

I'm unable to move. It's as though I've frozen. My whole body seems static although from the waist up, at least in my arms, there remains a slight mobility.

A roar of approval rises from the audience as she raises the axe and brings the silvery blade down on my right shoulder in a glistening arc. Muscle and sinew and nerves and bone are severed. My right arm hangs limp. The cheering from the audience - yes, they're cheering now - becomes deafening. There's laughter too. *Laughter?* It comes from the balconies.

I try to stop the scene like I was able to do in Phases One and Two. I can't. I try again. It's not possible!

I reach slowly up to my right shoulder with my left hand as if to heal the wound.

The pain is excruciating.

The axe falls again. It falls at an angle toward the side of my body. This time my left arm is hit at the elbow but the brunt of the blow is received by my chest, and I hear the cracking of ribs.

There is blood everywhere; on my body, on the stage floor, splattered up Annette's stomach and across her breasts. There is blood coursing down her legs.

But the axe seems blunt. It's as though the edge has been filed down and roughened so that the maximum damage will be done without severing anything completely.

The agony is unbearable as the axe swings against my left shin and the tibia splits. I want to fall to the floor of the stage but am unable to do so. The axe falls, over and over.

I'm screaming, I'm crying, I'm pleading.

Annette lowers the axe and reverses the blade.

I look down at the axe head. It is razor sharp. The edge is not blunted. It is sharp like a Samurai's sword. The steel is glowing grey and silver. Annette's expertise is responsible for what the axe blade severs and what it doesn't.

The audience cheers, they roar, they clap, they stamp their feet.

Annette smiles. She looks toward the audience as if asking for approval. With louder cheers they give it. She slides the axe between my feet then swings the axe upwards. Her aim at my crotch is perfect. It splits my coccyx.

I'm screaming, louder this time.

I feel the vertebrae splitting one by one, the os sacrum, L5, L4, L3, L2, L1. My pelvis is shattered into two pieces.

The pain is excruciating. The terror is unending.

My head is spared as Annette turns and walks away. She leaves me to my screaming.

The crowded auditorium erupts again in cheers and then, this time, in singing. I recognise the song, I'm sure I do, and want to join in but the pain is too intense. I believe it won't ever stop. The song is every song I ever knew.

But the pain does stop. There is no pain. The blood is gone.

The audience becomes silent and files out in perfect order.

Where am I? How did I get to wherever I am?

Incredibly, I'm in the middle of a stage, a concert stage; there is no proscenium arch, no curtain. I'm alone. There is no audience.

There is some music faintly playing...I think it's 'Dirait-on', by Lauridsen, one of my favourite pieces of music...

END